I0648860

United States Congress

Memorial addresses on the life and character of John G.

Warwick, a representative from Ohio

United States Congress

Memorial addresses on the life and character of John G. Warwick, a representative from Ohio

ISBN/EAN: 9783337200923

Printed in Europe, USA, Canada, Australia, Japan

Cover: Foto ©Raphael Reischuk / pixelio.de

More available books at **www.hansebooks.com**

HON. JOHN C. WARWICK.

MEMORIAL ADDRESSES

ON THE

LIFE AND CHARACTER

OF

JOHN G. WARWICK,

A REPRESENTATIVE FROM OHIO,

DELIVERED IN THE

HOUSE OF REPRESENTATIVES AND IN THE SENATE,

FIFTY-SECOND CONGRESS.

———

PUBLISHED BY ORDER OF CONGRESS.

———

WASHINGTON:
GOVERNMENT PRINTING OFFICE.
1893.

Resolved by the House of Representatives (the Senate concurring). That there be printed of the eulogies delivered in Congress upon John G. Warwick, late a Representative from the State of Ohio, 8,000 copies, of which 2,000 copies shall be delivered to the Senators and Representatives of the State of Ohio, and of those remaining 2,000 copies shall be for the use of the Senate and 4,000 for the House of Representatives; and the Secretary of the Treasury be, and he is hereby, directed to have printed a portrait of the said John G. Warwick, to accompany said eulogies. That of the quota of the House of Representatives the Public Printer shall set apart 50 copies, which he shall have bound in full morocco with gilt edges, the same to be delivered, when completed, to the family of the deceased.

Agreed to in the House of Representatives February 24, 1893.

Agreed to in the Senate March 2d, 1893.

2

ANNOUNCEMENT OF DEATH.

DECEMBER 6, 1892.

Mr. OUTHWAITE, of Ohio. Mr. Speaker, it has become my painful duty to announce the death of Hon. JOHN G. WARWICK, late one of our colleagues and a Representative in this House from the Sixteenth district of the State of Ohio. It is not my purpose at this time to make any remarks upon his life and public services, but I shall at an early day ask this House to devote a few hours to paying a proper tribute to his memory in hearing addresses from his friends upon this floor. I offer the resolutions which I send to the desk and ask their immediate consideration.

The Clerk read as follows:

Resolved, That the House has heard with profound sorrow of the death of Hon. JOHN G. WARWICK, late a Representative from the State of Ohio.

Resolved, That the Clerk of the House be directed to transmit a copy of these resolutions to the Senate.

Resolved, That as a mark of respect to his memory the House do now adjourn.

The resolutions were unanimously agreed to.

And accordingly (at 1 o'clock and 40 minutes p. m.) the House adjourned until to-morrow noon.

EULOGIES.

FEBRUARY 18, 1893.

The SPEAKER. The hour of 3 o'clock having arrived, the Clerk will report the special order.

The Clerk read as follows:

Resolved, That Saturday, the 18th day of February, 1893, beginning at 3 o'clock p. m., be set apart for the purpose of paying tribute to the memory of Hon. JOHN G. WARWICK, lately a Representative from the Sixteenth district of Ohio.

Mr. OUTHWAITE. Mr. Speaker, I offer the resolutions I send to the desk.

The Clerk read as follows:

Resolved, That the business of the House be now suspended that opportunity may be given for tributes to the memory of the Hon. JOHN G. WARWICK, lately a Representative from the State of Ohio.

Resolved, That as a particular mark of respect to the memory of the deceased, and in recognition of his eminent abilities as a distinguished public servant, the House, at the conclusion of these memorial proceedings, shall stand adjourned.

Resolved, That the Clerk communicate these proceedings to the Senate.

Resolved, That the Clerk be instructed to send a copy of these resolutions to the family of the deceased.

ADDRESS OF MR. OHLIGER, OF OHIO.

Mr. SPEAKER: The duty devolves upon me of paying a tribute of respect to the memory of my predecessor, the lamented JOHN GEORGE WARWICK. If as a neighbor and friend almost lifelong, if as a political coworker, I can suggest to this House some portrait of the Representative who disappeared from this earth only August last, I will be content.

JOHN G. WARWICK was born in County Tyrone, Ireland, December 23, 1830. When he had just about attained his majority he and a brother, who is still living, bid farewell to their boyhood home in that beautiful isle, that land of poetry and song, eloquence and wit, whose genial-hearted and sympathetic people have long struggled for liberty, and emigrated to the United States, tarrying awhile in Philadelphia, then pushed forward until the two brothers reached the small village of Navarre, in the proud Commonwealth of Ohio. He was not altogether without means, and yet at a meager salary became a bookkeeper in a dry goods establishment in that hamlet.

A few years afterward he moved northward, only about 5 miles, to the then very prominent canal town of Massillon, and there he was again employed as a clerk in a dry goods store. There are those yet living who recall his disposition, his methods of work, and industry at that early period of life. One can infer that he had an unusual ambition, an imbibed honesty that never departed from his mind, and a closeness of application which was one of the keys to his subsequent success in business pursuits. In a short time he became the successor of his employer and began the successful career in the mercantile line wherein he first engaged. Then he branched out into investments in flour mills and coal mines.

Coal is an abundant deposit in the region where he lived. He was an adroit investor, with the keenest perception of value and the probable output of mines, and in all other channels of business endeavor his shrewdness was displayed. He was a promoter of railroad construction, and his adopted city owes to his public spirit largely two of its valuable lines. He was a director at the time of his death in the Wheeling and Lake Erie Railroad. It was from an important meeting of this directory in New York he had just returned to this city when his fatal illness seized him.

He gave much attention to farming and raising of fine stock. With great nervous energy he directed his affairs, however much diversified. In this long business career the secret of his success was his rock-ribbed integrity. He discharged every obligation with utmost fidelity. He had accumulated at his death a large estate. When his early life is remembered the whole struggle furnishes but one more example of what brains, honesty, and persistency can accomplish in this free land. As long as I knew him it was never even whispered, even in the most bitter political campaigns, that JOHN G. WARWICK had ever, by act or intent, blurred the purity of his honest character. This much in brief as a sketch of the distinguished dead as a business man.

He early became interested in political action. He lived and died an undeviating and sturdy Democrat. His apprenticeship was served in the common council and the board of education. Gradually he impressed upon his district those combative qualities and shrewd management of campaigns which served him in later years when he was called to higher stations.

In 1883 he was nominated for lieutenant-governor of Ohio, and, with George Hoadly as governor, was triumphantly elected. It was a memorable canvass. The onslaught made upon Mr. WARWICK was unusually spirited. The most dangerous charge pressed against his candidacy was that he was an Orangeman. I trust it may not seem inappropriate to have recorded here that the charge was false. He was a man of singular toleration. Two years later the renomination came to the successful candidates, and though my dead friend received an advanced vote the whole ticket went down in defeat.

It was not for seven years that he again became a candidate for public honors. But in the interval he was always active, always liberal in contribution. He had a keen relish for political affairs. It was for him a delight to engage in the combats of parties, where friendship need not die, nor respect for divergent opinions be abandoned.

Mr. WARWICK was intense in his convictions, frank in their expression. He could not understand neutrality. There was no need to wait long for a discovery of what he thought. So incessantly did he espouse men or measures, with rare acceptance of compromise, that his real trait of fairness was often obscured. And yet he was nobly fair and generous. As in business, so in politics he had a controlling sense of respect for an obligation.

In 1890 there came the battle royal in the Sixteenth district of Ohio between himself and the now governor of Ohio, long an honored member on this floor. To the features of that campaign, as the daily prints have furnished its history, I have no wish to allude. It was a national combat that can not be lessened in its character or its vigor by any suspicion that those who participated are prone to exploit or exaggerate it.

It gave to the lamented dead great prestige and it was not ill deserved. To what impression he made during his brief career in this House it will be easier and more appropriate for those who knew him here to testify, but there are some characteristics to which in all sincerity I wish to pay my humble meed of praise. He was public-spirited, profusely charitable, and hospitable. No one in distress ever appealed to his sympathy and went away empty-handed; that great heart of his was ever seeking an object upon which to bestow a deserved charity. Many a young man starting in life felt the influence of his favor; he having fought the great battle of life successfully, knew its trials and loved to smooth the pathway of the young to success.

Many are the stories of his kind acts and charitable deeds. When the men in mines in which he was interested struck, and his partners advised that he furnish them no more flour from his store, his reply was characteristic of the man: "How can they have bread without flour? While I have flour they shall have flour." It suited his warm heart better to be duped than to turn away from what might be real want.

In his early youth he became a member of the Episcopalian Church, and in all church affairs he was often appealed to and, possibly, never refused the donation asked.

In his early youth Mr. WARWICK had received only the common rudiments of an education and at no time had the advantages of academic study. But as a young man he imbibed a masterful taste for reading, to which he yielded all his life. He was an omnivorous devourer of history and English literature; his mind had a peculiar bent for statistics, and he was an authority constantly consulted upon important questions.

There are many incidents in the career of my lamented friend that crowd upon my memory, but there are others here who wish to pay their tributes to him. After a brief illness in the capital, attended by his beloved wife and his dutiful son, his eventful life ended, and his spirit returned to the God who gave it. His death came as a great shock to his entire constituency, and the sorrow had about it none of the formality of royal mourning.

It was the genuine grief of people who knew and loved him. At his funeral were shown manifestations of the reverence in which his fellow-citizens had held him. Business was suspended. A long cortége followed his remains to the tomb. One scene, most touching, was the long line of four hundred miners, standing with bared heads in the blazing sun of that sad August day as the body of their loved employer was conveyed to the church. If, with measurable fidelity, I have drawn a portrait of JOHN GEORGE WARWICK as he was in life, a devoted husband, a loving father, an honest man, a benefactor of the poor, a faithful friend, I am content.

ADDRESS OF MR. JOSEPH D. TAYLOR, OF OHIO.

MR. SPEAKER: The death of the Hon. JOHN G. WARWICK, late a member of this House, to whose memory his colleagues and friends are met to pay tribute, is a vivid reminder of the uncertainty of human life. At the close of the last session of the present Congress he was in the full vigor of health and to all appearances had the promise of a long life. A few days before the close of the session he called at the Arlington Hotel, in this city, where I was then living, in company with the Hon. Daniel McConville, for the purpose of talking over a business enterprise, in regard to which he thought I could give him some information; and before leaving he arranged to go to Cambridge, Ohio, the town in which I reside, immediately after his return to his home at Massillon, Ohio, and I was to notify the parties he was to see at Cambridge that he would be there, and I did so; and before he got home, before he left this city, he was taken suddenly ill, and very soon the startling news came that he was dead. So sudden, so unexpected, it was hard to realize that it was true. The cares, burdens, and responsibilities of the long session, which had begun the early part of December, 1891, and lasted to the latter part of August, 1892, had been a continuous strain upon his nervous system. Few people who have had no Congressional experience realize the character of the work done, or the responsibilities assumed by a member of Congress.

The relief of the eight-hour system never comes to a member of Congress. His hours are the hours he can steal from constant pressure and constant demand. He does not belong to the district which he is supposed to represent. He does not belong to the party which elected him. He belongs to all districts, to all parties, to all parts of the country, to all classes, and must answer the demands of all, in every waking hour of the day, if not in the sleeping hours of the night. He belongs to the public, is the servant of the people, the tramway between the Government and his constituents, the responsible agent for all the ills of legislation.

This is the kind of life Mr. WARWICK had been living for nine months, and while he looked well and was apparently in good health his physical and mental powers had been severely taxed and his system had not the ability to resist the unexpected malady that befell him as he was finishing up his work in the national capital preparatory to going home. Death is always an unwelcome guest. It comes unexpectedly, comes before we are ready for it; but it seems harder in this case, because it came before he had reached his home; before he had the opportunity of once more meeting and greeting under his own roof his family and friends.

But the sad side of this picture is not the only side. The career of Mr. WARWICK is one which his constituents as well as his personal friends can remember with pride and gratification. As a citizen, as a business man, as a neighbor, and as a friend, Mr. WARWICK did his duty, and will be associated with deeds well done and with acts kindly remembered. He was honored and appreciated by his party, his State, and his country. He was elected lieutenant-governor of Ohio as a Democrat at a time when Ohio was regarded as a strong Republican State. He was elected to Congress over the Hon. William McKinley, jr., the present governor of Ohio, who was at the time regarded as one of the most popular men in the country. It is true that the district was Democratic, but his election at that time was regarded as a great triumph. And it should be remembered that he never surrendered to any constituency or to any party his personal independence.

He was a Democrat, but he believed in the principle of a protective tariff, and his influence was always exerted in holding back his party when he thought it was approaching too near the doctrine of free trade.

He was no extremist on any question. He believed in a wise and well-considered conservatism on all questions. In his home, in his family, in his business, in the senate of his State as its presiding officer, and in the Congress of the United States he was the same unostentatious, unassuming, plain man that we all knew when we knew him first.

He was born in Ireland in 1830, came to this country in his twentieth year, was elected lieutenant-governor in his fifty-third year, was elected to Congress in his sixtieth year, and died in his sixty-second year. His life swept quickly by, and what was a little while ago a living active presence is now with us only a memory, and it illustrates how transient and transitory are all the seeming realities of life. The sunshine of to-day gives way to the shadows of to-morrow. The joys of the present are supplanted by the sorrows of the future. This is the mysterious lesson of life and death; of time and eternity.

It is well, however, to note a worthy, useful, and successful life. Prominence among men is not to be lost sight of in weighing the attributes which make up a well-rounded life; but there is a character more to be commended, an ambition more to be admired—a faithful allegiance to duty and a conscience void of offense. And it is well to pause in this busy turbulent House long enough to pay merited tributes to the dead, whose vacant seats admonish us that life is too short to

be wasted in bitter wrangling or in partisan controversy.
Those oft-repeated words—

> Life is real, life is earnest,
>   And the grave is not its goal;
> Dust though art, to dust returnest,
>   Was not spoken of the soul—

express well the words of comfort that cheer the saddened
heart in the presence of the great shadow that falls so frequently athwart this Hall. But our friend and colleague is
not in fact dead. Though we speak of him as dead, the great
life that awaited him across the shadowy river is just begun.
Not only that, but the words he uttered here, the deeds he did
in his earthly career, will go vibrating and echoing down
through the ages to come. The spiritual forces and divine
influences of a noble life have no boundary this side of eternity. And the man who exerts these influences and makes
the most of life is to be held in grateful remembrance by a
grateful people.

The present Congress has stood around the open grave of
many of its members. Four Senators and ten Representatives,
fourteen members in all, have gone the way of all the living.
The funeral bell has scarcely ceased to ring, the sad requiem
of sorrow has scarcely hushed its plaintive notes, and Ohio has
had her delegation broken among the rest; but in the past
Ohio has been singularly spared this solemn experience. In
the ninety years of her history only one Senator and five Representatives have fallen at their posts of duty in the National
Congress prior to the death of Mr. WARWICK, and the last of
these five was my honored predecessor, Dr. J. T. Updegraff,
who died in November, 1882.

The great funeral procession, composed of the men whom he
had long employed, of the business men with whom he had
long transacted business, of his neighbors and friends, who had

watched his successful career from a man of moderate means to a man of large wealth, testified their high appreciation of his worth in life and their sorrow at his death. His success and usefulness in private life were more remarkable even than his efficiency in public life, and his whole career was without stain or tarnish.

No one could come in contact with Mr. WARWICK without feeling that he was a remarkable man, a man of marked ability, and a man of a high sense of honor, and his Christian character, his generous manhood, his home life and gentle manner made him a model worthy the admiration of the young men of this country. The country owes a lasting debt of gratitude to Ireland for giving us this worthy and eminent man.

There are other words of praise I should be glad to utter of my esteemed and honored colleague, to whom I became strongly attached on this floor; but I leave this to those who knew him longer and better than I did, to whom has been specially intrusted this sacred duty.

ADDRESS OF MR. ROCKWELL, OF NEW YORK.

Mr. SPEAKER: Could Governor WARWICK have known that these memorial services were to be held, he would have said, "Let there be no fulsome praise, no extravagant eulogy, and let no lips utter any but words of sincerity and truth."

For he was himself a frank and sincere man. He hated fraud and sham. He loved truth and sincerity. He knew his own powers and recognized his own limitations and he would have thanked no man for exaggerating those powers, or for crediting him with an absence of the weaknesses of our frail human nature.

He was a splendid example of the sturdy Irish Protestant

blood which has constantly enriched our country from its earliest settlement, and which has its exemplar in Andrew Jackson, between whom and Governor WARWICK were many marked points of resemblance. The same qualities of high courage, steadfast persistence, great personal independence, and warm and generous impulses, tempered by rare judgment, characterized them both. They each had the same fealty to friends, to party, and to any cause which they espoused. They were each strong in their likes and dislikes.

With Governor WARWICK, a friend once made was never abandoned nor neglected so long as that friend proved worthy of confidence, and a cause once espoused never failed to receive his entire devotion. Such is the estimate of his character which I formed from my acquaintance with him and my knowledge of his life and career. Before I knew him person-ally, he was the friend of my friend, devoting to his service an energy and zeal which won my admiration and regard, and this admiration and regard constantly increased as I came to know him better during our brief association as members of this House.

As I talked with him about the events of his active career, tracing him step by step from the humble Irish cottage in County Tyrone to his beautiful Ohio home; from his clerkship in a small country store to his position as the manager of vast business interests; from the small trader to being the employer of thousands of laborers, and from the immigrant ship to the halls of Congress, I became more and more impressed with his courage, manliness, and fidelity. He arrived upon our shores in 1850, a sturdy Irish boy of twenty years, with no capital save correct principles, a common-school education, and the great gifts of energy, perseverance, and unusual business apti-tude. He went at once to Ohio and soon after to the city which was his lifelong home.

Engaging in mercantile pursuits, his prudence and sagacity enabled him in a few years to purchase his employer's business. As he prospered he invested largely in coal lands and flouring mills, and later became largely interested in railroad enterprises.

He was from the start public-spirited and earnest in the promotion of the interests of his city, and was successively a member of its common council and board of education. As lieutenant-governor of his State, and presiding officer of its senate, he won the regard and esteem of every one without distinction of party.

His contest for election to this House against Governor McKinley and the strenuous exertions which were made to defeat him brought him into national prominence, and he came among us modestly wearing the laurels of a great and well-earned victory. He received the unusual recognition, for a new member, of the chairmanship of a committee. The same fidelity and zeal which characterized him as a business man were displayed in the discharge of his official duties.

The inborn love of liberty and of Democratic principles which caused him to leave his native land and become an American citizen continued to be his guiding star and made him a devoted member of his party. With him Democracy was a creed to which he gave steadfast adherence in prosperity and in adversity. He was no holiday soldier. His home life was happy. His last moments were soothed by the ministrations of his beloved wife and son.

The affectionate esteem in which he was held by his lifelong friends and neighbors at Massillon—his home for thirty-five years—was deeply manifested during his life and at his death. His unostentatious deeds of benevolence and charity had endeared him to thousands. As an employer he was just and generous. Four hundred of his employés, with bowed heads and moistened eyes, followed his remains to their last resting place, testifying in this manner their love and esteem. With the beautiful ritual of the church of his boyhood, to which he became connected before leaving his native land and ever after adhered, his body was consigned to the tomb—" earth to earth, ashes to ashes, dust to dust." " He rests from his labor and his works do follow him."

The great enterprises which he initiated still go on. His army of employés are still moving on in the steady ranks of industry, though under a new leader. But the land is more prosperous and thousands of its citizens are happier because of the life work of JOHN G. WARWICK.

I once stood beside the bedside of a friend whose life had been an eventful one. When told by his physician that he must soon die, he lay for a long time in earnest thought and then quietly said: "Well, I have made mistakes; but I have done the best I could." Happy will it be for us all if we shall be able to render such a verdict on our own earthly careers.

And I believe that Mr. WARWICK could not only have truthfully said this, but that he would have asked at the hands of his friends and fellow-countrymen no higher eulogy.

ADDRESS OF MR. CATCHINGS, OF MISSISSIPPI.

Mr. SPEAKER: I esteem it a great privilege that I am permitted to take part in these ceremonies. For our deceased colleague I entertained the most profound respect. Few men have possessed greater attraction for me. His campaign against so distinguished an opponent as the present governor of his State, and the great victory achieved by him, had given him national fame, and made him a notable figure in American politics before I ever met him. When the Representatives elected to this Congress began to assemble in this city in November, 1891, a natural curiosity to see and talk with the hero of that great contest, caused me eagerly to seek his acquaintance. His appearance was singularly striking and attractive. His face, to me, was unusually handsome, and bore marked evidence of the high and strong and manly character for which he was ever noted.

It may be it was because I instinctively associated him in my mind with his great and successful campaign that I thought of him as a soldier; and upon first seeing him I remarked to a friend that he looked like a field marshal. His manners were as attractive as his appearance. He impressed me as a man wholly free from guile, gentle yet strong, deferential yet self-respecting and courageous. A strong friendship soon grew up between us, and I often sought his society, and derived from it great satisfaction and pleasure.

His modesty is exemplified by the brief and simple biographical sketch furnished by him to the Congressional Directory:

JOHN G. WARWICK, of Massillon, was born in County Tyrone, Ireland, December 23, 1830; came to America in 1850 and engaged in mercantile pursuits; is interested in milling, mining, and farming; was elected lieutenant-governor of Ohio in 1883; was elected to the Fifty-second Congress as a Democrat, receiving 20,059 votes against 19,757 for William McKinley, jr., Republican, and 846 votes for J. J. Ashenhurst, Prohibitionist.

The career of the modest gentleman who gave this brief account of himself was one of which the highest and noblest might be justly proud. Coming to this country while yet a boy, with no adventitious circumstances to smooth his pathway, by his genius, superb judgment, and dauntless courage, he made himself the possessor of a princely fortune. And this was accomplished by such methods only as an honorable and just man may always employ. There were no short cuts, no doubtful practices, and, more than all, there was no grinding of the faces of the poor and the humble.

H. Mis. 104—— 2

All who knew him, rich and poor, haughty and humble, alike rejoiced in his prosperity, and loved and honored him. And as might have been expected of one such as he was, of the bounty that had come to him, charitable benefactions at all times and in many forms were generously, though unostentatiously, dispensed by him among those less fortunate than himself.

His election to the high and honorable station of lieutenant-governor of a great State, and his subsequent election to a seat in this House, bespeak the esteem entertained for him by his friends and party associates. Had he lived out his natural life there can be no doubt that still higher honors would have been bestowed upon him.

A good man, honorable citizen, and useful public servant has gone from us. His memory shall be affectionately and reverently cherished by me always.

ADDRESS OF MR. LAYTON, OF OHIO.

MR. SPEAKER: JOHN GEORGE WARWICK was born in County Tyrone, Ireland, December 23, 1830. His parents were poor people; his early advantages were few, and it was with but a meager education that he came to America, the land of his adoption, in the year 1850, with his brother Robert, who yet survives him.

After a short sojourn in the city of Philadelphia he removed to Navarre, Stark County, Ohio, where he secured employment as clerk and bookkeeper in a small country store. By strict economy and industry he was enabled a few years later to embark in business for himself in the city of Massillon, where he continued to reside until his death.

In 1865, while still at the head of a large and successful drygoods house, he became the owner of large and extensive flouring mills, and was the first to introduce new and modern machinery and improved methods of manufacturing flour in that locality. He soon thereafter became interested in and was selected and served as director of numerous railroads passing through that portion of Ohio.

He also invested extensively in real estate, and soon became the owner of several fertile and valuable farms near his home city.

Later on he invested extensively in mines also, and was one among the many large and successful coal operators of the State.

While engaged in the dry-goods business, which he disposed of in 1872, he was an extensive buyer and dealer in wool, and in this line, as well as in all others to which he gave his personal attention, by reason of his remarkable energy, careful business traits, and unerring judgment, he was entirely successful.

The value of his judgment in important business matters became so well and generally known that his aid and advice was frequently sought after by many other business men, and was always freely and frankly given. He was not only a man of sound judgment, but a man of strong convictions and fearless in their advocacy, and yet without malice, and reasonable in all things. He was also ever kind, charitable, and generous. Many a poor man, many an honest laborer, many a poor widow and orphan child will miss his thoughtful generosity.

While always a thorough, earnest Democrat, always taking a lively interest in the welfare of his party, he never sought office or place until the year 1883, when, yielding to the pressure of his numerous friends, who knew his sterling worth and character so well, he accepted the nomination for lieutenant-governor on the ticket with the Hon. George Hoadly for governor, and was triumphantly elected.

He presided over the senate of the sixty-sixth general assembly of Ohio, and, although devoid of any prior experience, yet, thanks to his good, sound practical sense and judgment, which always stood him so well in hand, he discharged his duties as such presiding officer, as well as those of the second officer of the State, in such a manner as to secure and retain the general admiration, esteem, and confidence of even his political opponents.

In the month of July, 1890, he was nominated by the Democrats for Congress in the Sixteenth Ohio district, having as his opponent on the Republican ticket Hon. William McKinley, now governor of the State. Notwithstanding the prominence of his opponent and hence the extraordinary efforts on behalf of the opposing political party to encompass his defeat, he was elected by a handsome majority as a member of this the Fifty-second Congress, where his merits were at once recognized by his appointment as chairman of the Committee on Enrolled Bills and as a member of the Committee on Public Buildings and Grounds, the first being an honor seldom, if ever, accorded to a new member.

In 1864 Mr. WARWICK was married to Maria Karthaus Lavake, an ever-faithful, worthy, and congenial partner, who, together with his only son, W. K. L. Warwick, survive him. And right here I may say that he was ever a kind, considerate, and affectionate husband and father.

He loved his good wife and son and ever merited the love and affection they bestowed on him in return.

On the 14th day of last August, 1892, at twenty minutes past 9 o'clock a. m., my friend and colleague, JOHN G. WARWICK, died at the Riggs House, in this capital of the nation, by reason of a sudden and violent attack of dysentery. His beloved wife and son were with him during his last illness, administering to his comfort with kind and loving hands, but neither their unremitting care nor the skill of his physicians could prevail against his acute disease. He was conscious to the end.

He was willing and prepared to die. His last words to them were words of comfort and love, such only as a good dying father can give to an ever-faithful and loving wife and dutiful son, whom he will meet in this world no more forever.

In his religious associations Mr. WARWICK was an Episcopalian, and was a prominent and liberal member of that church in his adopted city.

It is not by reason of any mere formal custom of this House that I desire to pay my humble tribute to the memory of JOHN G. WARWICK, but to perform a labor of love regarding one of whom I have for many years entertained the highest respect, akin to veneration.

I first became acquainted with him in 1883, ever since which time, notwithstanding the disparity of our ages, I was his friend, and I have reason to know he was mine.

And among my cherished recollections shall always be the thought, the knowledge, that I possessed the friendship of this modest, unassuming, yet strong, kindly, manly man.

His whole life history, from his boyhood days in that beautiful green isle to the hour of his decease, is that of intelligent effort and judgment and honorable conduct in its every detail. As a citizen, as husband, as father, as friend, he combined every element that is necessary to constitute each and all of them in their more perfect completeness.

His quiet, unassuming, and quaint ways, his ever-kindly, pleasant dealings, his liberal ideas, and bounties to the poor, needy, and deserving, his ever courteous and gentlemanly ways and manners in his daily walks, both in private and public life, endeared him to all with whom he came in contact, and his death has left a feeling of universal regret among all who knew him. The high moral character and noble, pure, and patriotic life of my friend remains not only a memory, but an imperishable legacy. A priceless heritage is that memory to his family and friends, who knew him best.

My acquaintance with my deceased friend was only made by gradual stages. He was not a man who sought intimacies among strangers, nor did he ever respond quickly to their advances. But with those who held his confidence, who, having the "Open Sesame," so to speak, to his big kindly heart, passed once within its recesses, he was like an open book; for them, for these, he "wore his heart upon his sleeve," ever full of kind, gentle, tender sentiments and deeds of charity and good will.

Fragment by fragment, while quietly conversing with him, I gathered from his own lips the story of his life; of his boyhood days spent in the green isle of his birth, amidst (almost) want, privation, and suffering on the one hand, and on the other (as he himself often said, as if he loved to dwell on the recollections of the place of his birth) amidst what always seemed to him as the greenest verdure, the clearest lakes, the brightest sky in any land; of his early struggles and more or less hampered efforts to obtain an education; of his patience and self-denial, so hard to exercise and endure by one in whose veins there flowed the fiery impulsive blood of his Celtic ancestors; of his arduous application to daily labor in inferior situations and employment until at last the bright sunshine of prosperity threw cheerful rays of golden light to cross his rough pathway; of his happy marriage in middle life and the long years of perfect bliss and enjoyment spent in the bosom of his family; of his business successes, earned by the hardest kind of work and closest application; of his final participation in civil and political affairs and his election as lieutenant-governor and then as a member of this honorable body.

The utter simplicity, the genuine modesty, the entire absence of boasting, self-emulation, and self-praise with which all these things were told to me was absolutely both novel and charming, and strongly but fairly outlines one of the prominent and lovable characteristics of my departed friend.

While it is true that other men under like disadvantages in early life have climbed from out of the valley of obscurity and poverty to the dazzling heights of fame and fortune, yet it is none the less to the honor and credit of my friend that he by his own unaided efforts and indomitable will rose from this obscurity and poverty in his lowly home in an oppressed and downtrodden land to wealth, prominence, social favor, and high political place among the highest and best of our nation's men. And this fact alone should and no doubt does solace and comfort his stricken family in their hour of distress.

He lived, as he himself said, in Ohio, his adopted State, because he soon learned to love her beautiful hills, her fertile valleys, her broad, rich plains, her many clear and beautiful streams, and her generous, kindly American people. As I have before stated, he made his home at Massillon, situated in a stretch of country of which may be said:

> No lovelier land the prophet viewed,
> When on the sacred mount he stood
> And saw below, transcendent shine,
> The streams and groves of Palestine.

He sleeps. My departed friend, JOHN G. WARWICK, now sleeps where the greater part of his simple, noble life was spent, his memory enshrined not only in the hearts of his immediate friends and neighbors, rich or poor, high or low alike, but of all who had the pleasure of his acquaintance.

He died in the harness while in the very midst of his work as a valued and useful member of this House.

His last work in this world is done and the record of his life is complete. Its pages are white as the driven snow;

and his history, from the cradle to the grave, is without blot or stain.   His name will not be forgotten until the history of Ohio has been obliterated forever.

Ohio, the birthplace and the home of many men, living and dead, of whom the nation is proud, has produced stronger, abler men no doubt; but if she has ever produced a better man in her modern days, it has not been my good fortune and pleasure to meet him.

With all his triumphs—

> Nothing in his life
> Became him like the leaving it; he died
> As one that had been studied in his death,
> To throw away the dearest thing he owned
> As 'twere a careless trifle.

His gentle voice is now silent; he will ever be missed from among us.   After life's labors so well performed he surely has received that highest reward of eternal celestial life.

As the poet puts it:

> He has done the work of a true man,
>   Crown him, honor him, love him.
> Weep over him tears of women,
>   Stoop manliest brows above him.
> For the warmest of hearts is frozen,
>   The freest of hands is still,
> And the gap in our picked and chosen
>   The long years may not fill.
>
>   *   *   *
>
> Never rode to the wrongs redressing
>   A worthier paladin,
> Shall he not hear the blessing
>   "Good and faithful enter in!"

ADDRESS OF MR. HARE, OF OHIO.

Mr. SPEAKER: It needed not the wisdom of Solomon to discover and declare the impressive truth that in whatever respects men may differ, whatever distinctions of birth or station, of talent or culture, of wealth or influence may have marked their lives, there is at last one event that is common to all.

To the monarch upon the throne as to the beggar at the palace gates; to the statesman crowned with honors as to the lowliest of his countrymen; to the scholar, the scientist, and the sage as to the unlettered serf; to the rich and powerful as to the poor and the oppressed; to all classes and conditions of men there is this common event in respect to which no man hath any advantage of his fellows, and which none may hope to escape by postponement to a day certain or indefinitely.

The very certainty of this event, the very fact that it is constantly transpiring about us and in our midst, tend to rob it of a portion of its terrors, and, by rendering us familiar with its presence, to render us also, in a large degree, insensible to the pangs it brings, to the wounds it inflicts, to the void it creates, to the loss and suffering it is almost certain to entail.

We are living in an age of great physical and mental activity; an age crowded with startling events; an age in which one great achievement "doth tread upon another's heel, so fast they follow," causing the world about us to pulsate with feverish energy, and to become restless with the spirit of enthusiasm enkindled by its constantly succeeding triumphs, and its anticipation of new victories in the swift-coming future.

In the midst of such surroundings as these we are apt to forget or neglect the duty we owe to cherish the memory and bear testimony to the worth and virtues of those with whom we have been associated here, but who have gone out from among us with their life-work completed, the record made up and the volume forever closed. Oblivion, Mr. Speaker, ought not to be the fate of any man deemed by his fellow-citizens worthy to be their representative in the councils of the nation, certainly not of any man who by his conduct here has honored the choice and confidence of his countrymen.

Hence, sir, whatever may have been said or written in disparagement of the custom we observe to-day in paying tribute to the memory of our departed associate, it is a custom not "more honored in the breach than the observance," and it is rendered all the more appropriate when the tribute we bring is in honor of such a man.

For, Mr. Speaker, JOHN G. WARWICK was not only a superior man, in that he possessed in large measure the essential qualities of true manliness, but the history of his life, should it be written, will furnish a most impressive illustration of the possibilities that are open to such qualities, to such a character as his, in this land of his adoption, and will thereby reflect honor as well upon his country as upon himself.

Born in County Tyrone, Ireland, the early years of his life were passed in that beautiful but unhappy country, where he acquired such schooling as was possible to a youth of his intensely industrious habits, and where under the guidance of his father, who was a merchant, he was made familiar with the rudiments of a mercantile education, and imbibed a taste for active business pursuits.

In the year 1850, before he was yet 20 years of age, he came to the United States, landing in Philadelphia. A stranger in a strange land, with no friendly hand stretched out to receive him, with no one to counsel or encourage him, with no capital but health, strength, intelligence, and determination to succeed, this young Irish immigrant encountered and proceeded at once to solve the same difficult problems that have been encountered and solved by thousands of his countrymen who have adorned with imperishable honor the history of their adopted country, and who to-day constitute one of the most valuable elements of its citizenship.

Tarrying but a short time in Philadelphia, his keen discernment pointed his course to the rapidly growing West, and he was shrewd enough to avoid the mistake so often made of losing his identity by seeking employment in the crowded cities of the seaboard.

In the selection of a proper location in the West he was equally alert and far-seeing, and was guided by the same discriminating judgment that distinguished his after years.

There is not to be found on the American continent a more tractive body of land or a region richer in all the diversified forms of material wealth than that embraced within the limits of **Stark County**, in the State of Ohio.

It was there that young WARWICK decided to establish his home. Entering into service as clerk in a store in the village of Navarre, he was able, by dint of the closest industry and economy, at the end of three years to enter into business on his own account in what has since become. largely through his efforts and enterprise, the thriving city of Massillon.

I shall not undertake, Mr. Speaker, to enter into the details of his remarkable business career. Whether as merchant, manufacturer, mill-owner, mine-owner, whether as the promoter of private or public enterprise, whether as an individual or in association with others, every undertaking in which he became interested seemed to prosper as if in response to the will of a master mind, as if in obedience to the touch of a master hand.

To him perhaps in as great measure as to any other citizen is the city of Massillon indebted for its past and present prosperity and for what would appear to be the sure promise of its future. For he was not only a pillar of strength in the maintenance and support of its varied industrial enterprises, but was as closely associated with its social life, with its charities, with its educational and religious institutions. He was, indeed, by common consent its model citizen.

Although a man of intense political convictions and always active and zealous in the discharge of what he conceived to be his public duties, it was not until comparatively late in life that he could be persuaded to accept other than strictly local public office.

In the year 1883 he was chosen to the position of lieutenant-governor of Ohio, and although without previous parliamentary experience, and perhaps with no taste or natural aptitude for the duties imposed upon him by his election to that high office, he nevertheless so applied himself to the discharge of those duties as to merit and receive the warm approbation of senators of all parties, and to firmly establish himself in the confidence and esteem of the people of Ohio.

Retiring at the close of his official term, he continued in private life until called to lead his party in a contest with one of the foremost statesmen of the country, a contest that will ever be memorable in that district, and which resulted in his election to the Fifty-second Congress.

His service here was brief, but honorable in the highest degree. Assigned to the chairmanship of the Committee on Enrolled Bills, and to a conspicuous place on the Committee on Public Buildings and Grounds, he brought to the performance of his duties the same conscientious, painstaking application, the same uncalculating zeal and fidelity that had distinguished him through life.

Perhaps no man who served here for so brief a period will be longer or more pleasantly remembered than will Governor WARWICK. At no time in robust health, but, on the contrary, a frequent sufferer from the disease which ended his life, he was nevertheless always cheerful, always cordial, always hopeful.

Although his countenance in repose bore the appearance of sternness and might convey the impression that he was of an unsocial and austere disposition, it needed only the approach and greeting of a friend or an acquaintance to cause it to light up with a smile so genial as to betoken a nature at once amiable and sincere. And that was his real nature. It was the quality which, united to a fine sense of honor and the most scrupulous integrity, drew to him not only the confidence but the esteem of all with whom he came in contact, and bound to him his legion of friends.

Nevertheless he could exhibit not merely the appearance but the quality of sternness when occasion required. He detested shams, despised hypocrisy, and did not always carefully weigh his words in characterizing the thing his judgment condemned, but in denouncing what he believed to be vicious in principle, or corrupt in method, he was both vigorous and unsparing. But he was never ungenerous—on the contrary, no man was more tolerant or more considerate of the opinions and feelings of his associates.

At his home in Massillon he was greatly beloved. Not alone in the estimation of his business associates and among those with whom he came into most frequent contact did he hold a high place, but throughout all classes of the community and particularly among the poor, to whom he had been a benefactor, whose homes he had often lighted and whose burdens he had helped to bear, his name was a household word, and the memory of his many unobtrusive acts of kindness will remain forever fragrant.

It was my sad privilege, Mr. Speaker, to accompany the body of our friend to its last resting place in the beautiful cemetery near by the city of his residence. If there could ever have been any doubt of the affection in which he was held by his neighbors, who knew him best, that doubt must have been dispelled by the evidences of grief that abounded on every hand. Owing to an accident the train was four hours late in arriving at Massillon, but during those four hours more than a thousand people had stood patiently waiting in the hot sunshine of an August afternoon in order to be present at the station when the train should arrive. All business was suspended. The great factories, employing hundreds of men, were closed in order that employers and employés might unite in paying the last tribute of respect and affection to him whose unexpected death was symbolized in the tokens of mourning that were visible everywhere.

It has been my fortune to be present at the obsequies of many eminent men, but I have never witnessed a more impressive exhibition of genuine, unaffected, universal grief than was manifest on that sad occasion.

On the previous day, at a mass meeting of the people of Massillon, this feeling had found expression in many forms, but notably in a series of resolutions, from one of which I quote such testimony as might constitute a fitting epitaph to the memory of a philanthropist:

Resolved, That in Mr. WARWICK we recognize a true and valued friend, a man of unblemished character, always kind and generous to the poor, of great and honorable skill in business, and strong and helpful in all public and private enterprises that secured the welfare, prosperity, and advancement of the city and its people. His death is a public calamity.

And this sentiment, Mr. Speaker, was but illustrated and emphasized in the unforced assemblage of the multitudes who, on the day of his burial, thronged the streets and stood with uncovered heads as the body of their friend was borne to the tomb. Such a demonstration as was there witnessed of the reverent grief of a whole city constitutes a more eloquent testimonial to the worth and virtues of our departed associate, and to the love and veneration of his fellow-citizens, than the most glowing eulogium of the most gifted tongue.

And if by those who, at most, bore to him only the relation of neighbor and friend the death of such a man was so deeply mourned, what shall be said of the grief of her to whom for so many years he had borne the tender relation of husband, and of her son upon whom he had lavished from infancy the indulgent love of a father? To the one remains only the priceless legacy of his memory as she walks in the gloom of a shadow that shall never again be lifted; to the other the example of a life and character such as the inspired writer must have had in mind when he declared "A good name is better than precious ointment, and the day of death than the day of one's birth."

The lessons of such a life ought not, indeed, to be lost upon any young man whose laudable ambition it may be to carve out from hard conditions the fame of a successful and honorable career. They ought rather to be pondered with serious and attentive care. For his was not an exceptional career saving to the extent and in the respects that it was rendered so by his own efforts and energy. None of the advantages of wealth or influence could be invoked to aid him in the outset of his struggle for recognition and success. No royal road was opened up before him; nothing but the same beaten path that stretches itself at the feet of every youth and is blazed throughout its entire course.

It is not the "primrose path of dalliance," nor is it always strewn with roses.

On the contrary, it is sometimes a rough and weary way, beset with thorns and brambles, and calling often for the exercise of the heroic virtues of patience, fortitude, and self-denial. But it leads always to honor and usefulness; often to fortune and fame.

And whoever will may pursue it without other guidance than the simple observance of the field notes that are blazed along its course.

Industry, economy, diligence, sobriety, integrity, these and their kindred virtues, justice and charity, coupled always with a generous sense of equity, and with that fidelity which keeps a man loyal and true to the very spirit and intent of the faith that may have trusted him without requiring at his hands the form of a promise or a pledge; these, sir, are the emblems that mark the path; these constitute the essential elements of true manhood, and without them success in its highest and best sense is impossible.

That JOHN G. WARWICK possessed and cultivated all these ennobling traits of character none who knew him would do him the injustice to deny, and they constituted the basis of his claim to the respect, esteem, and confidence of his countrymen.

Although he did not attain the age of three score years and ten, allotted as the span of human life, he had yet lived long enough to fill the measure of his early ambition and to accomplish more than is ordinarily achieved by men who, by reason of strength, attain the age of four score years.

Fortunate in finding a home in this favored land, fortunate in the opportunities that were given him to serve the country of his choice and of his love, fortunate in his business pursuits, happy in his domestic relations, rich in the love of his fellow-citizens, and just entering here upon a new service for which he was well equipped, forming new associations which were in all respects congenial, there were indeed many reasons why our friend should prefer to live.

But he was not afraid to die. To him the final summons brought no dismay, no apprehension, nor did it take him by surprise.

Fortunate as he had been in all the relations of his useful life he was hardly less favored in the circumstances attending his lamented death.

Conscious to the last moment, in full possession of all his faculties and of the peace that passeth understanding, life's labor done, he was ready to receive his reward.

And so, surrounded by those he loved and with a smile upon his countenance, he entered upon that dark voyage so full of mystery and yet so full of promise and prospect and faith and hope as to banish all sense of dread from the mind of him upon whose kindling vision the receding earth was only bringing more clearly into view the light that shone from the farther shore, guiding him on the way to his eternal rest.

Peace to his ashes, reverence to his memory, honor to his fame.

ADDRESS OF MR. CARUTH, OF KENTUCKY.

Mr. SPEAKER: In the Fifty-first Congress a new measure had been brought forward which affected in some manner or other the whole people. If enacted into a law it would enter, either to bless or injure, every American home. With the name of one of the Representatives of the people that bill will ever be associated. He was a man of high character, of strict integrity, of undenied patriotism. He thought he was right and believed he was acting for the best interests of the nation.

Fierce and bitter was the parliamentary battle that was waged, but the followers of this leader looked to him for advice and guidance, even as the "Old Guard" looked to and obeyed the first Napoleon. His opponents yielded to him the respect his character commanded, but with vote and voice they contested his theories of the rights of the Government and fought to the bitter end to defeat the cause he espoused. The battle

H. Mis. 104——3

ended and on the banner of the leader I have described perched the eagle of victory.

However, the biennial elections were at hand, and the defeated but not yet vanquished transferred the conflict to the hustings and to the polls.

The measure and the man were to be upheld or defeated by the ballots of the people. What would be the result of the combat? This was the all-absorbing question in every city, town, hamlet, and home in the Republic.

To the Sixteenth district of Ohio the eyes of the nation were turned, for from this district came the leader I have mentioned, and on the result of this contest there seemed to depend the fate of the measure and the man.

The opposing forces were led by the one whose memory we this day honor.

I would not mar an occasion like this by any political references. Suffice it to say that the measure was repudiated, and when the smoke of battle cleared away from the Sixteenth district of Ohio—after a conflict which was waged furiously over every inch of the field—it was seen that the young "Napoleon" had met his political Waterloo.

It was in that fight that the American people learned to know by name and reputation the Hon. JOHN G. WARWICK; but those who honored him were not strangers; they had known him in the daily walks of life, and had helped to elevate him to the second office in the gift of the voters of his State; they had seen him discharge with dignity and honor the functions of lieutenant-governor of the Commonwealth.

The fame of the battle he had fought, the great victory he had won, made him a conspicuous figure in American politics, and he was "the observed of all observers" when he took his seat as a member of the Fifty-second Congress. He laid no claim to oratory, nor sought to load the RECORD with his views on every subject, but modestly, earnestly, and quietly in committee rooms, in **the Departments, and in this Hall he** discharged with earnestness and zeal his duty to his people, **his party, and his country.** In his intercourse with his fellow-members **he was** courteous, considerate, and kind, and loved the society of the scholar and the wit. His conversation contributed to the knowledge of the one and the pleasure of the other.

You remember, Mr. Speaker, the intense heat of the last summer; how the people fled to seashore and to mountain to escape the heated city and to breathe the cool and health-giving air. The members of **Congress, in** the discharge of their duties, **were chained** to their desks and to this Hall, and here, true to his obligations, remained JOHN G. WARWICK, although **the** companion of his life, **she who divided his sorrows and** doubled his joys, had been **prevailed upon by him to seek for** awhile the seashore, on his promise to join her, and find quiet, **rest, and strength after the trials of** the long Congressional session.

This hope of **happiness was destined never to be realized,** for when **the gavel went down to** close the session he was stretched on a bed of illness, and this loving, devoted wife had been recalled **to his** side to minister to **his wants and** soothe his pain.

His colleagues hastened **to their homes, happy to be** released, glad to see once more their neighbors and their friends, **but, alas!** never more in life was JOHN G. WARWICK to look on the face of those who loved and honored him. **Death came** and beckoned him **away from the pains and labors of time to** the rest and **rewards of eternity. He heard the summons and** with a farewell word of love to his devoted wife he followed the grim messenger. All **was over; a useful life** was ended; a distinguished career terminated in the grave.

The career of JOHN G. WARWICK fittingly illustrates what can be accomplished in this country of ours. Born on a foreign soil, in County Tyrone, Ireland, he left the unhappy land of his birth before he attained his majority to find in this Republic more incentives for exertion and greater liberty of thought and action. A youth without advantages, a stranger in a strange land, with no means, he made his home in Ohio, engaged in mercantile pursuits, then in mining and farming, amassed a fortune, and died before he had reached the allotted "three score and ten," an honored and respected member of the highest law-making body in the land.

He accomplished this, Mr. Speaker, because he was a man of determined purpose, who in life knew no such word as "fail." Obstacles could not bar or impediments impede him if in the way of the object he desired to attain. Fixed of purpose, strong in his convictions, loyal and devoted in his friendships, loving and tender to wife and family, these were the predominant traits of character which marked his life.

Well may his people mourn the loss of one whose life contributed to the benefit of his kind. Well may his family weep over the desolation of a home his loving, thoughtful care made bright and happy. Well may the nation thus sorrow over the death of a patriot citizen who loved her institutions and contributed to her greatness.

ADDRESS OF MR. CALDWELL, OF OHIO.

Mr. SPEAKER: The House does well, even when affairs of state are closely pressing it, to commemorate the virtues of JOHN G. WARWICK. To pay the tribute of love and acknowledgement to a public man of his worth is an affair of state.

He was a part of this House, and the loss to us and to the

people when he died was so heavy that the memorial custom which has so long prevailed in this body has emphasis in his case.

One of the wholesome, indeed essential, elements in our beneficent and successful form of government is unceasing party contention. The life of a republic depends on the existence of political parties. With all men in agreement on all propositions, and with no minority to scrutinize and threaten, and even to mount and ride with power—with the people for an army—we should have a government no better than the effete systems. Indeed, the more earnest and combative the parties within the lines of peace the greater is the safety of the form of government we have chosen, for the people are thus stimulated to a consideration and understanding of public questions.

Every true and courageous man admires a partisan—he who has earnest convictions with the courage to proclaim them. Who advocates and defends his principles with honesty and enthusiasm is useful as a citizen or as a servant of citizens, no matter to what party he belongs. His virility entitles him to admiration and respect which we can not accord to the shuffler and trimmer.

The men who settle great questions and truly and honorably lead the people are the men with views and rugged fighting qualities. We have respect for an open, honorable adversary, who meets us point to point and foot to foot, and if defeated bows to the majority like a true American. It is one of the compensations of our system that we can shake hands across the party lines.

It does not require much time for the acute man to penetrate a Democratic or Republican uniform and discover a warm heart beating within. No longer, certainly, than it takes to prod the cold, repellent disposition.

Shakespeare wrote for all time and for all men. He indited words applicable to JOHN G. WARWICK when he describes the prince, who was "framed in the prodigality of nature." Nature was profuse to him with its gifts of sense, ability, devotion to friends, philosophic tolerance of the views of his opponents, and a generosity that was princely and absolutely unaffected.

Governor WARWICK passed sixty fleeting years on earth. He had almost attained his majority before he came to this country from Ireland, but he was of that composition which rapidly comprehends and appreciates free institutions, and he quickly became a typical American. He had the best education in the principles of popular government that a thoughtful and practical man could have—a self-education.

He differed with many of us in the details of legislation, but on the main issue his position could not be fairly questioned even by a political opponent. He was a patriot, a devoted lover of his country. In his modest way he was a statesman. Statesmanship consists not alone in towering oratory and learned treatment of abstruse constitutional questions; it is a term which ought to embrace the qualities of the man who, from a practical standpoint, perceives the precepts of a good government, and uses every effort, according to the light thrown upon him, to preserve and perpetuate that government.

Governor WARWICK was a power in any enterprise with which he was associated, in politics, business, or social life. He had great strength in his known soundness of judgment and his unquestionable probity. He always did what he believed to be right, and he was not moved to perform while there was the slightest question in his mind as to the honesty of the enterprise. He was a strong organizer and disciplinarian.

When he became an advocate of a measure in Congress. whether political or not, he was an active advocate. He was sleepless and relentless in promoting what he believed to be good and needful legislation. Once convinced of the justice and propriety of a measure, Governor WARWICK was a most valuable ally. His promise of support did not mean perfunctory words and a mere ranging of himself on that side. It meant activity and results. It meant argument, solicitation, and the influence of a man whose own integrity was a recommendation for whatever he advocated.

He was powerful in persuasion. His personal appeals to members were more effective than speeches. Within his party, on political issues, and in all parties on questions that were nonpolitical, he was almost irresistible. He was a commanding man. He believed in using the means legitimately at his command to secure proper results. He had a personality that was imperious when necessary, and gentle when gentleness was the proper method. He was a most valuable man in the organization and discipline of the party to which he was devoted, and the party opposing his views always felt the necessity of alertness when he was in authority.

He was to a great extent a WARWICK in the histrionic sense. He was the potent agent and desired the promotion of many men, and had much to do with the adoption of doctrines. He was tenacious. To enlist him in a cause was to prepare to fight it out to the end. He was not a compromiser; he always studied the ground so well and was so moved by his integrity, as well as his judgment, that he was past the compromising point before he entered the fight.

He was versatile in his methods. He had thoughtful things to say to those who were thoughtful; strong argument for those who were wavering; gentleness for those who were gentle and receptive, and stern command for those who were obstinate and obstructive. And, with it all, he earned such a high character for integrity and sense that he generally won on all lines.

Governor WARWICK was a successful man; success came to him not as a result of a mere spirit of gain, but as the reward of a wise, liberal, and unselfish policy. His prosperity was the prosperity of the community in which he lived. His example stimulated other capitalists and employers to do justice. He was a useful man. He developed natural advantages, built up towns, and built up men. His generosity to worthy young men seeking to carve out positions for themselves was one of his most beautiful characteristics. He helped himself and then he helped others. His genius led him on to honorable fortune, and his goodness of heart made others the beneficiaries of his success.

He once found himself, through his associations with other operators of coal mines, with his employés on a strike where their lack of employment soon left them without means, but they had unlimited credit at the store which the governor conducted. An attempt was made by other employers to discipline him for giving practical aid to the strike; but he had no sympathy with the starvation policy, and rebelliously declared that the men should have provisions from his store as long as he had any.

This, Mr. Speaker, was illustrative of the character of Governor WARWICK. He was a business man with whom other business men desired to have associations on account of his sagacity and integrity. But he was not sordid. Money-getting was not the chief end of his life; money was to him something desirable to have for the use there was in it. A colossal fortune in the hands of JOHN G. WARWICK would not have incited the unrest found among the people on account of the concentration of wealth. The cry of plutocrat could find no lodgment against him. What he had was employed for the betterment of the general condition.

The poorest man in his community was always glad to hear

that he had advanced financially, for that meant better times for all. There could be no better example of frankness than was furnished by the man we are honoring. He was absolutely unaffected. He was a plain, straightforward, honest man. He pretended nothing. He knew his compass and kept within it. He spread no sails on unknown seas; he knew what he could do and he did that well. He selected his sphere of usefulness with unerring judgment and became great in it.

What he might have been as a public speaker, had education and circumstances bent his mind in that direction, we can not, of course, tell, but that his work was as effective as oratory we know. He brought reason, force, and example to bear. He was gifted in persuasion and power; he was well fortified to meet either the thinker or the obstinate man. In behalf of a friend or in advocacy of a principle he was a soldier as well as a missionary. His zeal was great, but it was not blind. He knew in what fields to work. In the pursuit of an object he lost no time and he wasted no strength. He had in an eminent degree the faculty of knowing how to work in each case where an impression could be made, and where work could be of no avail.

Members of this House in daily association become impressed with the amenities of life. They discover that in the performance of their duties the acrimonies of party politics are only incidental. They learn that in things really necessary to do in the main, purposes for which they have been sent here, there is a common ground on which all must get together. There are honest differences every day, and in essential matters the antagonists of to-day may, on some other question, be working elbow to elbow to-morrow.

We meet in common in the committee rooms and are naturally thrown together much in the hours of rest and recreation; under associations of this kind no man can long conceal his faults, and no man, however modest, can long obscure his virtues. JOHN G. WARWICK bravely passed this test. In our midst he was an active spirit—was a working legislator, who kept abreast of current information; who loved fellowship; who was aggressive in promoting what he believed to be right; who was reciprocal when reciprocity was honorable and consistent, and who had the highest motives in his acts of kindness.

Being such a man he was well known to all of us, and knowing him as we did we honor his State, his country, and ourselves as much as we honor him in engaging in this memorial service.

Death is appalling in its frequency. The thoughtful man must shudder when he recounts the mortality even in this Congress. But, often as it may come, it is a duty we owe to ourselves, to humanity, and to the tenderest sentiments to pause and pay honest and loving tribute to him who has gone before us to an eternity whose unknowableness inspires us with awe.

We can well spare from the public business time to perform these offices which mark civilization and enlightenment.

Mr. Speaker, a life is not such a little thing that when it goes out we may discharge it from our memory and go on in uninterrupted worldliness. Death comes with a fresh shock every day. We can not get used to it. We wonder why, when there are so many less fair fields for devastation, it cuts off in the supremacy of his usefulness such a man as JOHN G. WARWICK. But we can only wonder and accept, and derive poor satisfaction from the poet who writes:

> The good die first,
> And those whose hearts are dry as summer's dust
> Burn to the socket.

The end of the worthy life of a good man conveys a greater lesson than can be expressed in words. It stimulates the faith of the ardent believer in a blissful future and arrests the cold philosophy of the skeptic. Whatever our reasoning may be, whatever material views we may take of the mystery that closes existence, so far as we know it, we find ourselves cling-ing tenderly, hopefully, and in faith to the thought that there is a better and greater life into which our honored friend has entered. To us left, in a brief battle with things mundane and at best but a span behind him, he leaves a gracious mem-ory.

ADDRESS OF MR. BENTLEY, OF NEW YORK.

Mr. SPEAKER: It was my good fortune to meet Governor WARWICK in the opening days of the first session of the Fifty-second Congress, and, as I lived at the same hotel with him all through the many months of that season, I enjoyed the rare privilege of a close intimacy and friendship with him. His genial personality and his steadfast integrity commanded the respect of all who enjoyed his acquaintance, while his great kindness of heart and sincerity of purpose and manner strongly intrenched him in the affections of his friends.

Men of genuine excellence in every station of life; men of industry, of integrity, of high principle, of sterling honesty of purpose, command the spontaneous homage of mankind. It is natural to believe in such men, to have confidence in them, and to imitate them. All that is good in the world is upheld by them, and without their presence in it the world would not be worth living in.

JOHN G. WARWICK was one of these men. From an hum-ble station in life he went forth to do battle with the world; to carve out a destiny for himself. He was inspired with an earnestness of purpose which was determined to win success.

Integrity, fidelity, and industry were the strong defenses of his early years, and never in all his busy and useful life was his honesty or the purity of his motives questioned.

Born in Ireland in 1830, he came to this country at the age of 20 years and soon engaged in mercantile business, where his energy, tact, and capacity early placed him in the foremost rank of the business men of the town of his adoption. Identifying himself with various public enterprises, he extended his business relations into the fields of mining, milling, and transportation. He served as a director in several railroads and was one of the chief promoters of the Cleveland and Marietta Railroad.

A consistent and aggressive Democrat and always a liberal contributor in means, in counsel, and in effort to the success of his party, he was always reluctant to become a candidate himself for any office, but finally accepted a nomination in 1883 for lieutenant-governor of the State of Ohio, and, being elected, he discharged the duties of that high office with a fidelity and ability which justified the confidence of his friends and won the esteem and commendation of his political opponents.

He was again nominated in 1885, but shared the defeat which came to the entire Democratic ticket. In 1890 he was nominated for Representative in Congress from the Sixteenth Ohio district as the candidate of the Democratic party against William McKinley, jr., and was elected after a contest which was one of the most memorable in the history of Congressional elections.

Taking his seat in the Fifty-second Congress, he brought to the affairs committed to his charge the intelligent industry and fidelity which always marked his business career. His courage, his strong will, his honesty of purpose, and his frankness of speech never left any one in doubt as to the position he occupied upon any public question.

No man more strongly possessed the characteristic of unswerving constancy to his friends. Never doubting, never fearing, he was always ready with a strong arm to lean upon, a true heart to confide in, and with instant response to every call that could be made upon his sympathy and devotion.

There was no room for cant, pretense, or hypocrisy in his nature. His pulse never beat with one false emotion. While we mourn his loss; while we miss his pleasant face, his gentle voice, his kindly manner, and offer our most affectionate tributes to his worth and memory, we may well pause at the threshold of the touchingly beautiful home life which has been enshrouded with the impenetrable gloom of a measureless sorrow.

It was there, in the tranquility of his home, where the spirit of love and duty wisely ruled, where the daily life was honest, sensible, kind, and loving, that he found his highest peace and happiness, and no one knew better than he, from a glad and bright experience, that earth holds no joy so sweet as the quiet contentment, the gentle, winning, confiding love, the serene and hallowed associations that cluster around the idea of home. It was in the daily tenderness and devotion of domestic life that the golden threads were wrought into the texture of his moral character, which gave him calm and peaceful entrance into the "beautiful home of the soul."

ADDRESS OF MR. HOUK, OF OHIO.

Mr. SPEAKER: I have been exceedingly gratified in listening to the eloquent and beautiful tributes that have been paid to the memory and character of our deceased colleague, Governor WARWICK. As my acquaintance with him only commenced with the beginning of this Congress, it was not such as to enable me to depict in such terms as have been employed by the gentlemen who have preceded me the qualities that have inspired such heartfelt and eloquent eulogies. I have therefore made no special preparation in submitting the few thoughts I have to express on this occasion.

Governor WARWICK impressed me from my first acquaintance with him as a gentleman of great sincerity and simplicity of character, kind in all his impulses, of great personal purity, and sterling integrity. I doubt not he discharged all the duties that were ever imposed upon him, in any of the relations of life, with conscientious and diligent fidelity, and with all the ability with which God had blessed him.

He was a useful man here. His worth was recognized by all with whom he came in contact. It is fitting that such a memorial ceremony as this, in accordance with the custom that has prevailed here for many years, should be observed.

A few thoughts have been suggested to me whilst listening to these beautiful tributes to the memory of our departed colleague that I will attempt briefly to express.

In looking around this Hall of the American House of Representatives, upon these seats, and galleries through which there has been passing a constant, never-ceasing flow of life for more than a quarter of a century, I am reminded of scores of eminent men whom I have known, and who have passed from the arena of terrestrial existence. Three of these distinguished men, Gen. Robert C. Schenck, Clement L. Vallandigham, and Lewis D. Campbell, were my predecessors as Representatives of the Third Congressional district of Ohio on this floor.

Among those recently deceased may be named ex-President Hayes, James G. Blaine, Gen. Butler, Samuel J Randall, and S. S. Cox, all of whom have left their impress upon the legislative history of the country. This stream of life flowing through this Hall, notwithstanding the constantly recurring withdrawal, one by one, from the membership of the House by death, is ever full; but how forcibly are we reminded, by this ever-shifting scene, of the sublime apothegm of Burke, uttered by that great orator when, during a speech on the hustings, he was informed of the sudden death of his competitor. He at once cut short his speech, gathered up his papers, and exclaimed with touching pathos, "What shadows we are, and what shadows we pursue."

And are we not all shadows? Are not those who have gone before us, and who during their terrestrial lives impressed themselves upon the history of the country, and contributed to shape its destinies, the realities?

Look upon the portraits of those two immortal patriots that adorn the walls of this Hall. There, sir [pointing to the portrait of Washington at the right of the Speaker's chair], is a character that is more vividly and widely impressed upon this nationality than any merely human personality has ever been impressed upon any people in human history. Everything around us here recalls the life, the name, and the services of Washington. And does he not still live? Does not the magnificent monument in sight of this Hall, that symbolizes the purity and dignity and simplicity of his character, testify to living and will it not testify to coming generations that he still lives?

And his companion there [indicating the portrait of Lafayette], who illustrated the bravery, the chivalry, the generosity of the French character in coming to assist in the achievement of our national independence, does he not, too, still live in the hearts of the living as he will forever in the hearts of future generations of the American people?

Mr. Speaker, there are other gentlemen who have asked and been accorded the privilege of adding their tributes on this occasion. I will not deprive them of that privilege by the use of any further time. I have only arisen to testify briefly my respect for the memory of this estimable and most pure gentleman, who was the first to be called from the membership of the Ohio delegation to the Fifty-second Congress, from the activities of this to the mysteries of the better and more exalted life.

ADDRESS OF MR. PEARSON, OF OHIO.

Mr. SPEAKER: Frequently, indeed, have the members of the Fifty-second Congress been called upon to pay their tribute of respect to the memory of a deceased fellow-member; and while on other occasions I have listened in silence and with interest to the words of praise spoken in behalf of such deceased member, I can not now preserve a silence which might be construed as a want of respect and love for him in whose honor these ceremonies are held.

While I had some acquaintance with Hon. JOHN G. WARWICK prior to our meeting at the organization of this Congress, yet I did not know of his real, true worth, until we became associated as colleagues from Ohio on the floor of this House. It was here that I learned to not only respect and admire, but to love the man. He was a true, manly man, full of honor and truth, bold and aggressive, yet modest and unassuming; a man of strong convictions, and earnest in maintaining them.

Governor WARWICK, as he was familiarly called by all who knew him, was loved and respected not only by the people of his Congressional district, but by the people of Ohio generally, and by all who were so fortunate as to know him intimately and well.

If there was one honorable trait in his character which deserves mention more than the many others it was his true friendship and gratitude. In all my associations with men I do not remember to have met any who surpassed him in this regard; once your friend, your especial friend, you could safely depend upon him under the most trying circumstances.

What a lesson the history of his life affords to the youth of our country; born upon Irish soil, he came to America when less than 21 years of age, and, in the midst of strangers, in a strange land, but in free America, where honor, integrity, and true worth are recognized, unassisted by friends of influence or wealth, he commenced, as it were, the battle of life alone; but by his honesty, his industry, and his untiring energy, he fought his way on and up, until he was elected by the people of his State as lieutenant-governor, and later honored with a seat on the floor of this House, both of which positions he filled with honor to himself and credit to his people.

Governor WARWICK held many positions of honor and trust, and in all of them it can truthfully be said of him that he discharged his duties faithfully and well; he realized that, in official position, he was but the servant of the people, and it was their interest he consulted in the discharge of all his duties. It was this devotion to their interest which so endeared him to them.

Mr. Speaker, I well remember the expressions of sorrow heard on every hand when the sad words, "Governor WARWICK is dead," reached the people of his adopted State.

As I have said, they had learned to love and honor him; they recognized in him a true representative of their interest, and hence they felt keenly the loss which, in his death, they sustained, and in many an humble home the silent sympathetic tear was shed, and a fervent, earnest prayer was offered for the widow and immediate friends of Governor WARWICK.

H. Mis. 104——4

ADDRESS OF MR. DUNGAN, OF OHIO.

Mr. SPEAKER: It was an ancient Thracian custom to weep around the cradle and to dance around the grave, mourning over the beginning of this troublous life, and rejoicing over the commencement of a higher life.

But we are more human in our philosophy, and rejoice when we have the great gift of one to love, and mourn when death claims a friend. And even in the deepest grief, how it comforts the stricken soul to recall the virtues, the kindnesses, the countless acts of love of the departed. And we do not so much mourn for the dead as we mourn for ourselves, for our loss, for the blank left in our lives. It is as natural to remember as to love, and since the days when David sang of Jonathan, his friend, mankind with one accord has done itself the honor to commemorate the virtues of the worthy dead.

To-day we dedicate an hour to the memory of JOHN G. WARWICK, of Ohio. Nor do we, his friends, want panegyric, but truth; for in this case the truth is highest eulogy.

Born in the little town of Grotan, in the County Tyrone, in Ireland, he became an American, not by accident of birth, but by the deliberate act of his young manhood he chose our country for his country, our flag for his flag, and our people for his people. Coming to the United States when 20 years old, he so acclimated himself to our institutions that for years he has been trusted with many public places of honor, connected with the management of the schools and municipal government of his adopted city, as well as in the wider field of State and national action.

Elected lieutenant-governor of Ohio he presided over the Ohio senate with the dignity of a simple, kindly nature. Afterwards, sent to this Congress in a most memorable contest with a great national leader of the Republican party, and then unanimously chosen as Ohio's member of the national Congressional committee, he remained always the same quiet, earnest gentleman it was his nature to be, and the Democracy of his chosen State never did itself more honor than when it honored such a man. And this generous-hearted man from a generous-hearted race, in making so good an American, never forgot to love and help his fellow-countrymen, for he was not only a splendid American, but a typical warm-hearted Irishman always.

His character can be easily described by those who knew him, for his life was an open book that might be read of all men. A clear-headed, prudent, but energetic man of affairs, with capacity to grasp the details and the possibilities of many kinds of business, he engaged in labor, in merchandising, in milling, in railroad building and operating, in coal mining, and in farming, and successfully conducted them all. His pronounced personal qualities were honesty, modesty, simplicity, sympathy, and generosity.

Can another star be added to such a crown?

Sincere and unassuming, full of kindness for the humblest man he met, kindness that not only felt, but helped; trusted by the rich and loved by the poor, none had ever sincerer, sadder mourners than he; one instance will show at once his kindness, his manly independence, and his simplicity. During a strike that stopped work at all the mines in his region, his own amongst them, he was requested to attend a meeting of the mine owners, and was there asked what he meant by supplying strikers with provisions from his stores during a strike. "Why," said he, "those people have dealt with me long, and always paid me; they have worked for me, and will again, and if I don't trust them for provisions where can they get any?" and that settled the matter.

The nation and the world have often to pause to say, "We have lost a great man," but we to-day do more than that. We stop the business of this House to mourn the loss of a good man—a true man.

To say more of JOHN WARWICK than is true would simply be to insult the memory of the man, himself so true.

But this much was just to say, and while we have all heard such memorial exercises lightly spoken of, I yet maintain that they have their high use to the living.

After the white blamelessness of sixty-two years of active, earnest, almost faultless life, he leaves a memory fully fit to be cherished.

The legend of St. Humbert is that that good man was buried with a green branch lying on his breast, and when a hundred years afterward they chanced to open his grave they found the body had become dust, but the fair branch, unwithered, still kept its perennial green. So with good men. They die and their bones turn to ashes, but long in the hearts of their friends the memories of the good they wrought abide imperishable. "For though dead they do live again. Their lives live after them." And it is well to stand for an hour by this bier and speak to each other of the dead, for there surely are men who when dead still live "to make the next age better than the last."

And the lives of many people are better—happier, and therefore better—because of JOHN G. WARWICK'S life.

We are better because we knew him, and we may be very sure that in the eternal mystery of death he can not be else than enjoying the reward of a life so full of good deeds done in the body.

We may not know where the loved who leave us go—

But this we know: Our loved and dead, if they should come this day,
Should come and ask us, "What is life?" not one of us could say.
Life is a mystery as deep as ever death can be;
Yet, oh, how sweet it is to us, this life we live and see.

Then might they say, those vanished ones, and blessed is the thought,
"So death is sweet to us, beloved, though we may tell you naught;
We may not tell it to the quick, this mystery of death;
Ye can not tell us, if ye would, the mystery of breath."
The child who enters life comes not with knowledge or intent;
So those who enter death must go as little children sent.
Nothing is known. But I believe that God is overhead,
And as life is sweet to the living, so death is to the dead.

ADDRESS OF MR. DONOVAN, OF OHIO.

Mr. SPEAKER: It is not inappropriate that I, a native of the State of his adoption, should pay my tribute of respect and affection to the memory of him whose presence within its borders for so many years did so much to make it a greater, a better, and a happier Commonwealth. His many noble qualities, his lofty understanding of his responsibilities, and his earnest endeavor to discharge promptly all his obligations will not soon be forgotten by the good people of Ohio, many of whom were the beneficiaries of his kindness and generosity, and all of whom, with bowed heads and aching hearts, lay their garlands of pathos and sorrow on the hallowed tomb of JOHN G. WARWICK.

I first became personally acquainted with him at the organization of the present Congress, and although he was 29 years older than I, a lasting friendship soon sprang up between us. I learned to admire the sturdy virtue, the persistent energy, and the unflinching honesty of my friend and colleague.

He was born and reared in the sacred land of my ancestors, and possessed the frankness, generosity, and courage characteristic of the Irish race. His abhorrence of despotism and his love of our free country and its institutions, impelled him at the age of 20 years to bid farewell to his native isle and seek a home in a land where kings do not rule by the grace of God.

He possessed good judgment and business sagacity in an eminent degree, which, with his gentlemanly deportment and unquestioned honesty, soon made him a favorite in social circles and a prominent man in commercial affairs. He believed that in our system politics and the economic problems involved therein are inseparably connected with our business and social life; and he deemed it not only a privilege to ·be enjoyed, but a sacred duty to be discharged, that every good citizen should be well informed on all questions of civil government and political economy, affecting the welfare of the people and the safety of the Republic.

Mr. WARWICK was a thorough Democrat and labored zealously and effectively for the ascendency of the principles of the party with which he affiliated, and in which he had an abiding faith. He was a consistent but not a bitter partisan, and believed that while a candidate for public office should be loyal to his party, a public officer should be loyal to the people.

It is not surprising that such a man should be sought as a political leader; indeed it would be surprising if he were not so sought. In the year 1883 Mr. WARWICK was nominated by the Democracy of Ohio for lieutenant-governor, and was elected. As presiding officer of the Ohio senate he was patient, fair, and just, and won the confidence and esteem of the members of that body irrespective of party affiliations.

After one of the fiercest and most memorable campaigns in the history of Congressional elections, Mr. WARWICK was elected in the year 1890 to represent the Sixteenth district of Ohio in the Congress of the United States. During the all too short time that he served as a member of this body he proved himself an active worker, a prudent legislator, a patriotic citizen, and an honest official. His associates and coworkers on both sides of this Chamber join me in bearing witness that our lamented colleague deserved all the encomiums that have been pronounced on him and was worthy of all that has been said eulogistic of his many virtues.

No greater panegyric can be delivered on any man than to say that he is an honest American citizen. JOHN G. WARWICK was an honest citizen of this great Republic, and for his indubitable loyalty to it the people of the whole country owe a debt of gratitude to him, the sanctity of whose ashes is preserved by commingling with its sacred soil.

ADDRESS OF MR. OUTHWAITE, OF OHIO.

MR. SPEAKER: So much has already been said to commemorate the virtues and perpetuate the good name of our late colleague that I feel unprepared to make any important additional contribution to these ceremonies. But my high esteem for Mr. WARWICK and my sense of the loss which this House and the State of Ohio sustained in his death impel me to add a few sentences of tribute to his memory.

Before he came here as a Representative of one of the most progressive, prosperous, and intelligent constituencies in Ohio he had won a high place among the citizens of the whole State. He was a self-made man who had impressed upon his neighbors and a wide circle of acquaintances the forceful integrity of his character. With but the ordinary groundwork of an education in his youth, by a careful and a zealous course of reading he had amassed a wonderful store of general information.

He was a close student of history and fond of English literature. He had collected a choice library as he pursued his work of self-education, and had learned how to use it to the best advantage. He was remarkably full of statistical information, especially such as related to important political questions. To facts concerning the promotion of the industries of mining and manufactures he had given much attention, and was a close observer of the operations of commerce.

To the learning found in books he had the valuable experience which comes from contact with all sorts and conditions of men. He was a large employer of labor, and had the constant regard of those in his employ. He had also received the general culture which comes to men as a result of travel, for he had visited many parts of this country, and met leading men in all the channels of life, as well as visited his native land and other portions of Europe. The story of his successful life is one of simplicity.

Starting in business life as a clerk in a little country dry-goods store, he became in mature years prominent in mercantile pursuits, as well as the operator of considerable coal mines, the promoter of manufacturing enterprises, and the owner of extensive farms. He gave to every work he undertook the most careful attention and zealous industry. He owed his success to this fact, and the further fact that his native prudence, sagacity, and industry was supplemented by the strictest integrity and fidelity to his obligations. These characteristics of his private life were intensified when he came to the performance of his public duties.

When lieutenant-governor of Ohio he held the respect of every member of the senate by the fairness of his rulings and his unfailing courtesy. When he entered the Halls of this Congress he came well equipped with information upon public affairs, anxious for the success of the political principles he adhered to, a prudent adviser upon party measures, and full of the patriotic purpose that all he should seek to do might be for the welfare and prosperity of the whole country and the happiness of all the inhabitants thereof. He made no pretensions to oratory, but in assemblies of citizens, in conventions and municipal bodies he often talked forcefully and fluently. His manner of speech was plain, blunt, cogent, and condensed. He made a sort of sledge-hammer presentation of cold facts and strong arguments.

During his last memorable campaign, which resulted in his election to Congress over the Hon. William McKinley, the only personal opposition urged against him was that he could not make a speech. At a great meeting of his party where he was present on the stand, held in one of the cities of the district, such cries were shouted. Mr. WARWICK deliberately came forward upon the platform facing the vast audience from whence such challenge had come and unmercifully rebuked this unbecoming treatment and proved his ability to talk to the point in a very few moments. After his election he made a trip to the Pacific coast, and while in San Francisco he was tendered a reception by a vast concourse of generous Californians. Upon this occasion he made an address upon public questions which was widely and favorably commented upon.

Mr. WARWICK was a thoroughly domestic man, fond of the retirement of his own home circle, and yet he delighted in the companionship of other men, had a lively sense of humor, and was a good listener. He enjoyed good stories and had a fund of them from which he drew to illustrate, entertain, or instruct. He was always a true friend, and was noted for his kind ways and benevolence. The affection felt for him in his home city was general, and his name was frequently sought to head subscription papers of a charitable or benevolent character. The poor of his city were greatly indebted to him and warmly cherished his memory.

Let me repeat one instance of his generous wisdom. Once, when a strike was going on at one of his mines, fully con-

vinced of the correctness and justness of his own position, he
could not forget that the families of his employés might suffer
while the questions of difference were under discussion and the
men without work and wages, and he sent them flour and grocer-
ies. In the end they yielded to his views. At his funeral
many hundreds of these same miners stood with uncovered
heads for about an hour in the hot sun to pay tribute to his
memory, while here and there tears moistened the eyes of
these true mourners for the loss of such a friend, a just tribute
to the good heart of our late colleague. He has earned a
golden page in the history of this country.

. ADDRESS OF MR. GANTZ, OF OHIO.

Mr. SPEAKER: The life and character of the late JOHN G.
WARWICK have been so appropriately and eloquently presented
by those who have preceded me in these memorial services that
there seems to be nothing for me to add, yet I desire to pay
tribute to the memory of my late colleague and friend. I first
made his acquaintance about ten years ago at the time that he
was a candidate for the office of lieutenant-governor of the
State of Ohio, and I was then much impressed by his undaunted
courage, his sincerity, and his lofty integrity. Fearlessly he
advocated his views and the tenets of his party, and by his
earnest, sincere manner he proved to be a tower of strength in
the political contest of 1883.

While not an orator, he exerted a remarkable influence, for
his positive manner and frankness of speech carried conviction
everywhere. He was not reared in the lap of luxury, but
unaided he fought his way step by step, until by unremitting
toil he attained wealth and honor. He filled the position of
lieutenant-governor with great credit to himself and his State,

and in the fall of 1890 was elected as a member of the Fifty-second Congress.

Serving with him during the first session of that Congress I became better acquainted with him, and learned to honor and admire him for his rugged honesty, devotion to his friends, and the many manly virtues which he possessed.

There never was a more generous friend, and all who knew him will join me in bearing testimony that his was a faithful, enduring friendship.

Strong to his likes and dislikes, he was an earnest, forcible champion of the cause of a friend, but always fair and honorable in dealing with an opponent.

The people of Ohio had the fullest confidence in this plain man, and it was with profound sorrow that they heard of his death. It has been truthfully said that the sorrow for the dead is one from which we refuse to be divorced, but I believe that the poignancy of that sorrow is and should be lessened and relieved by the consolatory knowledge that the departed one filled his mission on earth as God intended, and that the world is better for his having lived.

I am fully convinced that my friend and colleague always endeavored to do his duty earnestly and honestly, and that he was inspired in all his actions by motives of justice, patriotism, and purity; and certain it is that he missed no opportunity to make others happy. There can be no better test of a man's merit than the esteem in which he is held in the home circle, and in this Mr. WARWICK was everything that a loving and devoted husband and father could be, and enshrined himself in the hearts of his family so that time will not efface therefrom the memory of him who is absent, but not forgotten.

Any description that I could give of the many good and noble traits of character of the deceased would be incommensurate with the merits of him whom we all loved, and in whom

all who knew him had implicit confidence. But JOHN G.
WARWICK is no more, and while we miss him in this Chamber, he is also missed in the State of Ohio, and because he
was a kind father and a loving husband, he is sadly missed in
the home circle; but we may all be comforted in some degree,
because we know he has left behind him an honorable record
and a noble name.

ADDRESS OF MR. HARTER, OF OHIO.

Mr. SPEAKER: It is a privilege to be allowed to speak, even
if very briefly, of the man whose life and character are now
before the House for truthful comment and therefore for eulogy,
for the truth about JOHN GEORGE WARWICK necessarily
takes the form of commendation and the tone of eulogy. I
shall not ask much of your time, as a more complete review of
his career is very properly within the privilege of the honorable gentleman who, coming from the same State, now repre-
sents the district which sent Mr. WARWICK to the Congress
of the United States.

Born in the same county in which Mr. Warwick spent over
forty years of his life, my knowledge of the man and familiarity
with his career continued down to the hour of his death.

The private life, social character, and business relations of a
man largely indicate what will be his career after being called
into the public service, and brief and untimely as was the
record of Mr. WARWICK at Washington it promised to bear all
the fruit which a pure life and an honorable career among his
Ohio neighbors, beginning away back in 1850, foreshadowed.

In all the years I knew him I never heard him charged with
falsehood or dishonesty; the head of a large business, constantly connected with important enterprises, he won the name

of an upright merchant and an honorable and capable administrator of trusts, and when death reached him he enjoyed the confidence and held as firmly as any other part of his estate the esteem of those who knew him best.

No trait in his character was more distinctly apparent than a sympathy for others, which was almost boundless, and which in his long life showed itself in numberless deeds of kindly charity. In the city in which he lived he will be long missed by the poor and the unfortunate, and his place among the prosperous can not easily be filled. So far as he saw his duty before him, he did it, and more can not be said of any man; and happy will be those we leave behind us if, when the time comes for writing our epitaphs, so fair a scroll can be placed upon our tombs as the most unflattering and least eloquent of his friends here in this House declare to be due to JOHN G. WARWICK.

ADDRESS OF MR. SCOTT, OF ILLINOIS.

Mr. SPEAKER: The grim destroyer does not respect persons in reaping his rich harvest. When he cut down the Hon. JOHN G. WARWICK, of Ohio, he took one of nature's noblemen.

A brief acquaintance during the first session of this Congress was sufficient to enable me to estimate fully his high character. It was impossible to come in but casual contact with this true man without becoming his sincere admirer.

He was chairman of one of the committees on which I had the honor to serve. In this capacity I came in close contact with him and we became fast friends. If to know him so briefly and yet to form so strong an attachment for him, what must have been the enduring relation existing with those with whom he associated for a lifetime?

Coming into Congress as a new member, he at once assumed that station to which his natural abilities, strengthened by long public service in his State, entitled him.   Ever true and loyal to his friends he had their closest confidence.   He was always ready to serve them to the extent of his ability.   Having traveled extensively and being a great reader, he was fully abreast of the times in which he lived.

This tribute, though brief, is yet meant to express a sincere admiration for one who in life was an upright, able, and dignified gentleman.

ADDRESS OF MR. BRETZ, OF INDIANA.

Mr. SPEAKER: As the successor of Governor WARWICK on one of the important committees of this House, I come to offer my tribute of respect to the departed.

Of his life and character in detail I know nothing.   My first acquaintance with him was formed at the assembling of the Fifty-second Congress, and as the first session of that Congress progressed my acquaintance with Governor WARWICK grew more and more intimate.

As has been said of him, he was not quick to put himself upon intimate terms of friendship with new acquaintances; but his force of character so impressed those with whom he came in contact that it was a pleasure to seek and cultivate his friendship.   He was a man possessed of sterling qualities, frank and positive in all he said or did, and it is no great surprise that he rose, in a short life, from a penniless boy with a limited education to a man of some means, and attained the high distinctions he did in the political arena.   So forcible were these rare qualities of sturdy honesty that he was accorded positions on committees by the Speaker of this House rarely attained by new members.

The news of his untimely death was a great surprise to me, when I remembered that it had been but a day or two since I had left him in this city to go to my home, at the end of a long session of Congress, apparently in vigorous health; but the shock produced by the news of the death of our friends is sometimes somewhat lessened when we remember that many thousand years ago it was truthfully said:

"Man that is born of a woman is of few days and full of trouble. He cometh forth as a flower, and is cut down; he fleeth also as a shadow, and continueth not." "Thus wastes man! To-day he puts forth the tender leaves of hope; to-morrow blossoms, and bears his blushing honors thick upon him; the next day comes a frost, which nips the shoot, and when he thinks his greatness is still aspiring, he falls, like autumn leaves, to enrich our mother earth."

So it was with the deceased; while engrossed with the busy work of this life he was stricken down and suddenly there was heard the rustle of a wing and the soul of our esteemed colleague took its flight into eternity.

Mr. Speaker, no eulogy we can now pronounce upon his life can add anything to his already well-made record. His name and fame will adorn the pages of the history of his State, and when the historian recites in after years the past events of this great nation, the name of JOHN G. WARWICK will not be missing.

His deeds are accomplished, his name inscribed on the Book of Life; peace be to his memory; green be the grave where sleeps our departed friend. Let us hope that he is better off than those of us who survive him.

ADDRESS OF MR. HAYNES, OF OHIO.

Mr. SPEAKER: At the close of the first session of the present Congress I parted with my friend and colleague, JOHN G.
WARWICK, in this city. At that time he was seemingly in
good health and spirits, and told me somewhat of his plans
and purposes on returning to his home after the adjournment
of Congress.

The district which he so ably represented having been
changed after his election to the Fifty-second Congress it
seemed to our friend that there was no important public nor
party necessity demanding that he should make further sac-
rifice of his business interests, and he had, several months
prior to his death, advised his personal and party friends that
he would not be a candidate for reëlection as Representative.

He was satisfied and happy in the thought that he could
hereafter devote his time, means, and energy to developing
and promoting business enterprises which he believed would
greatly benefit, not only himself, but the people generally of
his town and district.

A few days after our parting it was with deep sorrow and
regret that I learned of Mr. WARWICK'S illness and sudden
death in this city.

I had known Mr. WARWICK personally for many years, and
intimately since 1883, when he was the nominee of his party
for lieutenant-governor of Ohio on the ticket with George
Hoadly for governor. He was elected by a large majority,
his popularity especially with the labor vote of the State aid-
ing materially in the success of the ticket. He made an envi-
able record as lieutenant-governor of the State and president
of the senate, retiring with the good will and esteem, not only
of his party friends, but of his political opponents.

Mr. WARWICK was a man of marked character and ability. Coming to this country when a young man of about 20 years of age, possessing nothing more than an honest heart and willing hands, he made his way to honor, distinction, and wealth.

In the discharge of his public duties, as well as in the management of his business affairs, he left the impress of his individuality on all his undertakings and his associates.

A kindly, genial gentleman; courageous, loyal, and true to his friends and trusts, positive in his convictions and earnest in the defense and support of party and personal friends. He was also a man of exceedingly kind feelings and impulses; generous, charitable, sincere, and earnest, he intended to do what was right to friends and opponents.

Mr. WARWICK was devoted and loyal to the political party with which he affiliated. He was a man of positive and strong convictions on questions of public or party policy, and always careful, painstaking, thoughtful, and efficient in the discharge of all public duties.

He represented his constituency faithfully and well; his good judgment, industry, and interest in the duties pertaining to a member of this House made him a valuable associate to his colleagues in this Congress.

While it is not my purpose to recount the details of the life of our friend—leaving to others to speak of his early life; his great labor and struggle to overcome the difficulties that surrounded his youth and early manhood; of his success in business; of his generosity and charity; of his happy home life and surroundings; the good will and confidence of his neighbors—I wish only to add that Mr. WARWICK has been identified with the business interests of his city and district for many years, always contributing his full proportion of money, time, and labor to the development and prosperity of the community.

H. Mis. 104——5

He was recognized in his city and district as a successful business man of great ability, respected and trusted implicitly by all, and the trusted friend and counselor of his neighbors and friends—a trust that was never betrayed.

I attended the burial of our friend and colleague, in the beautiful cemetery in the busy and enterprising city of Massillon, his home for many years. The shops, mines, **and business** places were closed, all work was suspended, and the long lines of workingmen, mechanics, **miners, and citizens, who** had stopped their labor and assembled to attest their **respect** and **sorrow at the death of their friend who had, for many years,** been their adviser and counselor, and their sympathy **for the wife and son who had been bereft of a** loving and devoted husband and father, told to all who were present that a man loved, honored, and respected had passed away forever.

Mr. OUTHWAITE. Mr. Speaker, other gentlemen desired to speak on this occasion, but are detained by illness or other **causes.** I therefore ask unanimous consent for leave to print, and that these gentlemen be allowed to submit their remarks.

There was no objection.

Mr. OUTHWAITE. I move the adoption of the resolutions.

The motion was agreed to.

Accordingly, in pursuance of the terms of the resolutions, the House (at 5 o'clock and 20 minutes p. m.) adjourned until Monday, February 20, 1893, at 11 o'clock a. m.

ADDRESS OF HON. ROBERT E. DOAN, OF OHIO.

Mr. SPEAKER: We have all been shocked and pained at the mortality among members of the two branches of Congress. How true it is that—

> To our graves we walk
> In the thick footsteps of departed men.

During the Fifty-second Congress fourteen members have been called to lay down life's burdens and answer the eternal roll call. Had the custom prevailed in this House of wearing the usual emblem of mourning for thirty days, we would have had a constant reminder that death is in our midst, and that this is indeed a house of mourning.

What a deep, sad lesson is conveyed to us in such a solemn hour as this. When old age has dimmed the bright luster of an active mind, when the zenith of capacity has been reached and passed, and we near the foot of life's hill, we bow in submission to nature's claims. But we stand with awe in the presence of death, when lips are silent that but yesterday pleaded with the impassioned eloquence of strong manhood, or when its withering touch fells to the bier a man in the full possession of all his powers, busied in the ceaseless activity of a useful life.

> What shadows we are, and what shadows we pursue.

How forcible, how significant, how impressive are the words of Watts, as they come ringing in our ears:

> Princes, this clay must be your bed,
> In spite of all your towers;
> The tall, the wise, the reverend head
> Must lie as low as ours.

Mr. Speaker, the life of JOHN G. WARWICK on earth is ended. His friends and country are left to mourn his loss.

Death can move from earth our friend, blot out all physical existence, but it is powerless to destroy the results of his labor, the impressions he has left, the good he has accomplished.

These are legacies of glory over which death has no power. In the well-directed life they comfort us like a living presence, and grow brighter and brighter as we descend the hill of life to sleep at its foot.

While there is no mystery like death, there is no theme so sublime and grand as immortality.   Blessed truth!

Fruits fall to the earth and decay, but never a fruit that did not leave its seed, and never a life that did not leave its example.

The sun of man's life goes down, but the star of his example remains in the firmament. The sun may set in the western sky amid the storms of earth, but it leaves a legacy of glory to the very clouds that obstruct its setting, speaking a language to our souls of a brighter day, a resurrection day, a coronation day, when God will gather His jewels in the eternal sunlight of His love.

Governor WARWICK was a Democrat of the old school.   He was a thorough disciplinarian; he was honest, conscientious, sincere, and true to a fault.   What he advocated he believed, and his very sincerity made you his friend.   The demagogue he despised.   The basis of his political action was that of absolute justice, and his motto was "That it were better to fail in the right than succeed in the wrong."   While you differed with him politically, you admired his frankness and probity.

In all his official acts as a member of the House, upon the floor, in committee, or in debate, he was the same sincere, candid, manly man.   In his death the country has lost a faithful public servant—the members of the House a conscientious co-worker in every department of legislation. As a citizen he had the respect of those who knew him best, without regard to party affiliations.   As a neighbor he was obliging; as a friend to the poor he was large-hearted, liberal, kind, and true.   No deserving man was ever turned away from his door empty-handed.   While he was firm and positive in his business matters and in his convictions of right and duty, he was nevertheless gentle in his disposition and ever anxious to add to the "sum of human joy."

I have not risen, Mr. Speaker, to deliver a eulogy on the deceased statesman. I shall not attempt to sketch the honorable steps by which he ascended to distinction in his own State, and obtained the confidence of all as a member upon this floor. That has been well and appropriately done by his colleagues and friends in this House. The deceased has made that task easy for—

The record of a noble life is that life's best eulogy; the history of the deeds of worthy men their most lasting epitaph.

I have risen simply to say a word or two in behalf of a worthy colleague from my own State of Ohio, and to render a tribute to his memory that is so justly deserved. In the general sorrow over his untimely death, I want to add the deep feeling of my own heart and drop a tear of sympathy and sorrow with those who loved him best in his own State and in his own home.

In these lessons remember God speaks, and—

To the dead He sayeth: Arise!
To the living: Follow me!
And that voice still sounding on
From the centuries that are gone,
To the centuries that shall be!

PROCEEDINGS IN THE SENATE.

ANNOUNCEMENT OF DEATH.

Mr. BRICE, of Ohio. Mr. President, I ask that the resolutions of the House of Representatives in regard to the death of my late colleague in that body be laid before the Senate.

The VICE-PRESIDENT. The Chair lays before the Senate resolutions from the House of Representatives, which will be read.

The Secretary read the resolutions, as follows:

IN THE HOUSE OF REPRESENTATIVES, *December 6, 1892.*

Resolved, That the House has heard with profound sorrow of the death of Hon. JOHN G. WARWICK, late a Representative from the State of Ohio.

Resolved, That the Clerk be directed to communicate a copy of these resolutions to the Senate.

Resolved, That as a mark of respect to his memory the House do now adjourn.

Mr. BRICE. Mr. President, I offer the resolutions which I send to the desk.

The VICE-PRESIDENT. The resolutions will be read.

The Secretary read the resolutions, as follows:

Resolved, That the Senate has heard with deep regret the announcement of the death of the Hon. JOHN G. WARWICK, late a Representative from the State of Ohio.

71

Resolved, That the Secretary communicate this resolution to the House of Representatives.

Resolved, That as a mark of respect to the memory of the deceased the Senate do now adjourn.

Mr. BRICE. Mr. President, at some future time I shall ask that a day be fixed when appropriate tributes may be paid to the memory and services of my late colleague in the other House.

The VICE-PRESIDENT. The question is on agreeing to the resolutions submitted by the Senator from Ohio.

The resolutions were agreed to unanimously; and (at 1 o'clock and 2 minutes p. m.) the Senate adjourned until Monday December 12, 1892, at 12 o'clock meridian.

EULOGIES.

MARCH 3, 1893.

Mr. BRICE. Mr. President, I desire to call up the resolution of the House of Representatives relative to the death of Hon. JOHN G. WARWICK.

The PRESIDENT *pro tempore.* The Chair lays before the Senate the resolutions of the House of Representatives, which will be read.

The Secretary read the resolutions, as follows:

> IN THE HOUSE OF REPRESENTATIVES, *February 18, 1893.*
>
> *Resolved,* That the business of the House be now suspended that opportunity may be given for tributes to the memory of the Hon. JOHN G. WARWICK, lately a Representative from the State of Ohio.
>
> *Resolved,* That as a particular mark of respect to the memory of the deceased, and in recognition of his eminent abilities as a distinguished public servant, the House, at the conclusion of these memorial proceedings, shall stand adjourned.
>
> *Resolved,* That the Clerk communicate these resolutions to the Senate.
>
> *Resolved,* That the Clerk be instructed to send a copy of these resolutions to the family of the deceased.

Mr. BRICE. I offer the resolutions which I send to the desk, and ask that they be read.

The PRESIDENT *pro tempore.* The resolutions will be read.

The Secretary read the resolutions, as follows:

> *Resolved,* That the Senate has heard with profound sorrow the announcement of the death of Hon. JOHN G. WARWICK, late a Representative from the State of Ohio, and tender to the relatives of the deceased the assurance of their sympathy with them under the bereavement they have been called to sustain.
>
> *Resolved,* That the Secretary of the Senate be directed to transmit to the family of Mr. WARWICK a certified copy of the foregoing resolution.

73

ADDRESS OF MR. BRICE, OF OHIO.

Mr. PRESIDENT: In paying tribute I can but indicate a portion of the respect and honor in which, in common with our people, I personally held the late Representative WARWICK. I can not, under the circumstances which now surround us, properly convey to you or to the Senate the full measure of his worth as a man, a citizen, a friend, and a Representative. We have now reached that stage in the session which deprives me of the opportunity and the power to express what I myself feel.

He was my friend for many long years. He was a representative citizen of our State for more than thirty years and one of its best known public men for more than one-half that period. He died in the confidence of his neighbors and friends. He died in the full vigor of his life, after he had been victor in a memorable contest which had made his name, for the time at least, national. The result of that contest placed him in the House of Representatives and put him in such a position in that body as fixed its attention upon him, upon his talent, upon his bearing, upon his character. He bore well in every respect that scrutiny, and he had not been a member many months until he was honored, admired, respected, and loved there as he had been at his home and among his people.

Mr. President, on August 14 of the present year the Hon. JOHN G. WARWICK, a Representative in Congress from the State of Ohio, died at the Riggs House, in this city. His illness was of short duration, and the deceased himself was the first to become aware of his approaching end. The members of his immediate family had been summoned, and in his expiring moments he had the consolation found in the presence of those who had been dearest to him in life.

The memory of Congressman WARWICK as a public man and as a private citizen is still fresh, and yet it will be a melancholy pleasure to recall the incidents of his memorable career. He was a marked type of the public-spirited citizen, and his kindly generosity in the affairs of life deserve a higher praise than I am able to bestow upon this occasion.

JOHN GEORGE WARWICK was born in County Tyrone, Ireland, December 23, 1830. His father was a merchant. In 1850 he came to the United States, and, after a short sojourn in Philadelphia, removed to Starke County, Ohio. In this community for forty years he found the scene of his life's endeavor.

In no man's history can the possibilities of energy and business integrity find a more striking example. First he became engaged as clerk in a dry goods store, and by perseverance and industry finally entered into business for himself upon a small scale. He possessed the shrewdness and tact characteristic of the people of his birth, together with a directness of purpose and skill in management which advanced him rapidly in the pursuit which he had chosen. His experience as clerk in a country store gave him an insight into human nature and a knowledge of the plain and rugged side of life, the impressions of which lasted until death. In the conduct of his affairs he was undeceived by pomp and ostentation, and always had a friendly hand extended in aid of deserving need.

When he had fairly established his footing in the community which he adopted as his permanent home he found himself able to embark in more ambitious enterprises. He gradually invested in many undertakings, and was remarkably successful in them all. During his career he was not only active in several large railroads, but was an extensive miller. His coal mining interests were large, and he gave much attention to his farms. The great secret of his life's success was his punctilious adherence to every obligation, and his enthusiastic and unchanging devotion to every enterprise into which he entered.

It was not in business affairs, however, that he exclusively took mental exercise. While a young man he had devoted himself eagerly to the study of American and English history, and in after life he was an authority upon nearly every event relating to the two countries whose annals he had so carefully studied in his youth. The diversion of reading was one of the fixed habits of his life, and the newspapers of the day were always to be found at his hand. It is not surprising that he was invariably abreast of the current of public affairs.

While building up his private business Mr. WARWICK did not seek political distinction. This came to him later in life, when he had more leisure and a greater opportunity to give attention to outside interests. He had accepted some local offices of minor importance, but it was not until 1883 that he became a well-known figure in the politics of his State. In that year he was nominated by the Democrats and elected lieutenant-governor of the State on the ticket of which Hon. George Hoadly was the head. He presided over the State senate for two years with marked ability and fairness. Upon his retirement from that position he was favored with the esteem of all who had come in contact with him as a presiding officer.

The next occasion upon which he entered actively into politics was in 1890, when he was the Democratic nominee in what was then the Sixteenth district of Ohio. The campaign was the most vigorous and hotly contested of that year, either in the State of Ohio or elsewhere. He had the honor to defeat a distinguished opponent after a canvass that attracted wide attention throughout the country, and which has since had an important bearing upon national issues. His success in this struggle did not go unrecognized. When he entered upon his Congressional duties he was given assignments of marked consequence in the body to which he had been elected.

His career in Congress was brief, but by no means unproductive. He had served only through the first session when he was lifted from the scene of his earthly achievements by the unkindly hand of death. However, within the brief period that fate accorded him for the service of the public in a Congressional capacity he accomplished much. The interest he felt in his own State and the particular constituency which he represented made him a watchful, wise, and earnest public servant in their behalf. Enjoying as he did the good will and confidence of those with whom he was associated, he used the opportunity for the greatest benefit of his country and his State. He was faithfully at his desk each day, and watched with unvarying care the changeful phases of national legislation.

He was unhesitating in expressing his opinions upon public questions, and his straightforwardness and courage in advancing his beliefs were always a source of strength to the causes which he espoused. Pretensions to oratory he did not make. In the few public addresses made by him his arguments were plain, cogent, unmistakable statements, requiring no interpretation to make clear their purport. In private conversation he had the same directness of manner, which gave him a force that he might never have enjoyed had he been the slave of ornate and effusive speech.

Full of humor, much of it of the sparkling kind attributable to his Irish birth, fond of the society of his friends, and with the mantle of charity always at hand for the failings and faults of others, no more companionable man ever shed the glow of human fellowship within the circle of his immediate friends. It is within that circle that his loss will be most fully measured.

In every respect Mr. WARWICK was a remarkable man. In

his struggles from poverty **to independent wealth the key of his success was his absolute integrity, perseverance, and native shrewdness.** The turmoils of business and politics he did not allow to disturb the serenity of his temperament. **His views of** party animosities, the rivalries and jealousies of daily **life,** were invariably tempered by tolerance. **He looked at the hamperings** of this world with composure. **Oftentimes he would** step from the scene of his active work and find rest and **recreation** in his books. It was thus that he sustained the equability of his emotions, notwithstanding the quick and energetic character of his mind.

Mr. President, I have but sketched **the history and qualities of the deceased.** An adequate **estimate of** his **worth is the** measure of grief that has been poured out by loving friends upon his tomb and the sense of vacancy that they feel now that **he is** gone. These are the tributes to which I would call your attention, and not to my **own inadequate expressions. The** memory of his character **serves as its highest eulogy.** In life he courted no undeserved praise; in death, no flower amid the **many blossoms dropped upon his casket fell from an insincere** or flatterer's hand.

ᐧ ADDRESS OF Mr. DANIEL, OF VIRGINIA.

Mr. President: The genius of Ireland, it seems to me, has found its most ample, generous, and brilliant expression in our own land. **We often hear our country** spoken of as the **greater Britain. It is just as truly** the greater Ireland. We learn of Irish statesmen and Irish soldiers when we **read our** school books. We catch the music of Irish **poetry in every** volume of essay and history or disquisition. **The brilliance of** Irish wit we find in the local **columns of our papers, and**

repeated from lip to lip in jest and converse by the hearthstone; yet if we were to judge of Irish character only by that which we hear of it as it comes to us borne from that distant land, we should have but a partial and imperfect appreciation of that people.

In our own country the name of the Irish soldiery has become a proverb of valor, and the brilliant generals who have borne it on every field have added even greater glory to it as it came to us by tradition. In literature too, and statesmanship, we have seen in our own country exemplifications of Irish genius.

And there is one feature of Irish character of which we could take but little cognizance except by our own experience, and that is the successful ability with which that race copes in our history with every circumstance which it has to combat.

We not only find the poor and humble Irishman with his pick and spade climbing the mountain and building the railroad, but we find him the president of the bank, the president of the railroad, the organizer of great commercial schemes and political movements, showing that Irish ability in business, where cold intellect meets its like in the hard conflicts of competition, is on a par with its brilliance as it shines in song and in story.

We know very little, Mr. President, of the details of the struggle of Ireland for home rule, and we know scarce any of it in the sense that we know our own political struggles and conditions; but the fact that the Irishman in this country shows constant progress wherever you find him, whether in the field of manual or intellectual toil, intensifies the belief that some peculiar condition of oppression must exist which has prevented him from becoming so independent and so great in his native land as he has become in our own. In the Old World the Irish orator might say of his countrymen: "They have fought successfully in every battle but their own." In this free country they have fought in all our conflicts of civic competition, and in none better than their own.

Mr. President, it is a privilege to pay a tribute of respect and honor to the worthy dead, and now as the hours of the Fifty-second Congress wane, we have paused to commemorate the virtues of one who entered it with us but did not live to see its close—a distinguished representative, who illustrated alike the genius of his mother Ireland and the great opportunities for the rise of merit afforded by his adopted land.

I did not have the pleasure of even a personal acquaintance with Mr. WARWICK. I do not know that mine own eyes have ever rested upon his face, but a circumstance of name attracted me to take particular notice of his political struggles and his marked career. He bore a name to me ever venerated, that of my own grandsire, John Warwick; and, while I have no reason to believe that we were kindred, it led me to make frequent inquiries concerning him.

In this manner I became familiar with the general reputation which Mr. WARWICK bore, not only as a public man but as a citizen in the community where he lived. That fixed reputation, which was attested not only by the public prints, nor only by the voice of his political friends, but by every manner of communication from all classes of men who had known him in all relations, is his best praise. One account has always been given of him, and that is that he was a man amongst men, universally esteemed, greatly confided, trusted, and believed in.

So he enjoyed that greatest proof of a man's worth which comes from the collected judgment of men who know him in all relations and all conditions, and now he lives "in a people's voice, the proof and echo of all human fame."

There were certain qualities of Mr. WARWICK which appear to have been as well known and recognized as his name. They were modesty, integrity, charity, and ability. There is such emphasis sometimes put upon the declaration that a man was " honest " as to convey an undertone of suggestion that the virtue is rare. It goes without saying that the public men of our country are honest. The lack of honesty in them is very, very rare. It would be a great reproach to our people and our free institutions if such were not the case. The hazy lights of political literature are often misleading.

There is no more honest or straightforward body of men in the world than those who represent the American people in public life. They are in the blaze of popular inspection; and if their qualities or actions are sometimes portrayed in distorted lights, and if there be occasionally some one that does not deserve the name, it is nevertheless true that in no other walk or profession, whether it be mercantile, legal, scientific, or otherwise, are there more proportioned to their number who deserve the name of honest than the statesmen whom our people have entrusted with power.

When I speak of Mr. WARWICK as a man of integrity, I do not mean simply to say that he never took his neighbor's goods, nor slandered his good name; I mean to signify that he impressed upon all who knew him the fact that he was punctilious in the observance of every obligation—mercantile, social, political, or otherwise. His charity has been borne witness to by too many testimonials to need circumstantial relation. His ability has been attested by many and varied accomplishments. His must have been a diversified order of genius. He was a merchant, he was a farmer, he was a miller, he was a miner, and he succeeded in whatsoever he undertook.

The public position which he won was through the confidence

he had inspired amongst the **people with whom** he lived, by his diligence and by his success, and by the character he had manifested in that success. Public honor was but the manifestation of that broad appreciation of his State which sent forth a representative man—representative in his sterling virtues as well as in his political opinions, **to** utter its thought, and do honor to its character.

Mr. President, the saddest phase of public **life is found in** the partings which it leads to, and I know not sometimes whether those partings be more sad when they are with the dead or the living. We are but brief sojourners here, **at best, whatever** may be our fortunes in life; and although many, **not** to say all of us, are partisans, all partisanship is merged **in the friendships formed by community of** service for a common **country, and by the** sentiments inspired when we stand by the dead forms of those who have been our **fellows.**

Changes of administration are well **for** the **public** weal. **Experiment can not test the rival claims of men and** measures except **through their agency. It is the crucible of ideas** and their **champions. But whether** on one side or the other of political difference, **whether of** victory or defeat, the change severs strong **and tender ties and** breaks cherished associations and foretokens the great change when all shall pass the common way.

JOHN G. WARWICK has only passed before us in the procession. He has lived his life, he has done his work, he won with **virtue the laurel that now lies** upon his tomb. Those who yet press **on** the toilsome march find refreshment in his good example: "Let him boast who putteth his armor off, not him who putteth it on" is now the conqueror's boast for him. Clean, bright, without tarnish, the armor which he wore is now hung **up as the relic of** him who wore it well; and **Ohio** receiving his dust may be proud in the realization that he whom she honored so often has honored her in turn by his useful and unblemished life.

The PRESIDENT *pro tempore.* The question is on agreeing to the resolutions submitted by the Senator from Ohio [Mr. Brice].

The resolutions were unanimously agreed to.

www.ingramcontent.com/pod-product-compliance
Lightning Source LLC
Chambersburg PA
CBHW032353020726
47499CB00008B/2723